THE KID!

A shadow moved—a thin silhouette leaped into the glowing doorway.

"It's the Kid!" a dozen voices cried, and the stabbing yellow fingers from twenty rifles jabbed at him.

He ran through the leaden holocaust with death snapping viciously at his heels. Ducking, twisting, nothing seemed to touch him. The crowd had been too eager; they were guilty of mass reflex fire—jerking their triggers with buck fever. Billy had a Colt in each hand and his small clenched fists exploded as he went across the yard in a running crouch.

To the Western scholars and researchers who sifted the Facts from the Fantasy—Ramon F. Adams, J.C. Dykes, Maurice G. Fulton, J. Evetts Haley, William L. Hamlin, Frazier Hunt, William A. Keleher, Robert N. Mullin, and Philip J. Rasch.

THE TRAIL
OF
BILLY THE KID

by
Robert Edmond Alter

WILDSIDE PRESS

PROLOGUE

Billy the Kid rode across the New Mexico territory and into American folklore; and he will probably continue to ride on and on through one decade after another until he becomes so obscured by an accumulation of sensational legends that in the end he will appear only as a mere wisp of a myth totally lacking in flesh and blood substance.

He has already very nearly reached that ghostly stage.

In the eight and a half decades since his death his brief life has been so exaggerated and romanticized that we are now close to the point of losing sight of the real man. Magazines, books, movies, television (even a ballet!) have all done their best to create a dramatic and distorted image of Billy the Kid which is so contradictory that we cannot help but get the feeling we are looking at two entirely different people.

Billy has been called everything from a Western Robin Hood to a psychopathic killer. In his case the truth *does not* lie somewhere between the two. He did not rob the rich to feed the poor, nor did he deliberately gun down twenty-one men in cold blood. In reality he was a homeless young cowboy who suddenly became entangled in a vicious range war. He fought on what he thought was the right side, and he fought to save his life. It was as simple as that.

The *Legend* of Billy the Kid originated in the nimble brain of a somewhat crackpot itinerant printer named Ash Upson, who in the course of his erratic career was slightly involved in the Lincoln County War which made Billy immortal. Fascinated by all the violent participants who passed his door Upson decided to write a romance about the most outstanding figure. He called his book *The Authentic Life of Billy the Kid*. It was about as authentic as the story of Washington chopping down the cherry tree.

The discovery that he lacked many of the vital statistics for his "authentic" biography was no problem at all for Ash. What he didn't know, *he made up*, and the myth spinners have been adding to his creation ever since. Thus today we can thank the fertile imagination of these legend workers for all the erroneous information we have regarding the life of Billy the Kid.

Ironically, the few outstanding "facts" that most modern Americans know about Billy are all pure fiction . . .

Billy the Kid's name was not William H. Bonney.

He did not kill twenty-one men (one man for each year of his life).

He did not kill his first man at the tender age of fourteen to protect his mother's honor.

He was not a bank bandit or a stagecoach robber or a holdup man in any sense of the term.

We do not even know where or when he was born. According to legend, it was in a New York tenement building on November 23, 1859. But this again was an Upson "fact." Let it ride; it's possibly close to the truth. Evidently Billy never said anything to the contrary during his short and violent life.

What *is* known is that his father's surname was McCarty, and Billy the Kid was born with the name Henry McCarty (How fortunate for American folklore that he later decided to change it! Picture such titles as *The Saga of Henry the Kid* or *Henry McCarty, Boy Outlaw*). Supposedly the father died when Billy was three and Mrs. McCarty and her two small sons (Joe McCarty was Billy's older brother) moved out West.

It is on record that Catherine McCarty married a William H. Antrim on March 1, 1873, in Santa Fe. This Antrim was an easygoing drifter of thirty who worked at being a miner, tinhorn gambler, and part-time butcher. After his marriage to Billy's mother he moved his ready-made family to Silver City in the southwest area of New Mexico. It was there that Catherine Antrim became ill with what was then called "galloping consumption," and she died on September 16,1874.

According to those who knew the Antrims the stories concerning Billy and his mother were true. He adored her, and her sudden death caused a great trauma in his adolescent personality. It did not embitter him against the world, but it did serve to give him a deep sense of futility. Why fight so hard for survival when everyone was slated for a relatively quick death? His mother had been only thirty-four years old. The young McCarty boy became a fatalist. What would be would be.

His lackadaisical stepfather did not seem much inclined toward rearing his foster sons properly and the job of caring for the two motherless boys fell upon kindly neighbors. Young Billy found a temporary refuge in a Silver City hotel as a waiter-dishwasher but he couldn't see much future in it and soon gave it up.

It was a wild period, set in a wide-open frontier town, and the endless procession of miners, cowboys, gamblers, gunslingers, dance-hall girls and Mexican *vaqueros* dazzled the impressionable fourteen-year-old boy. He wanted to be a vital part of the rip-roaring times. Dropping out of school he began to round out his dubious education in the saloons and gambling dens. No one seemed to care much one way or another.

Though only semiliterate the boy was already a great favorite among the Mexican inhabitants because he could rattle off "border Spanish" like a native, and being a likeable little cuss the grub-line riders and frontier gamblers took to showing him their tricks with guns and cards. He soon learned how to handle both with deft precision and was seriously thinking about becoming a professional monte dealer.

About the only problem he could have had at that point of his colorful life was the confusion regarding his name . . .

Some called him by his real name, Henry McCarty, and some called him Henry Antrim, while still others referred to him by his stepfather's name, young Billy Antrim. At the same time he was also known simply as the Kid, and this evolved into Kid Antrim and Billy Kid.

There is an old story that his famous pseudonym came about in this manner: A few cowboys were sitting around a campfire and one of them idly asked, "Where's Billy?"

"Who?" another wondered.

"You know," the first cowboy said, "young Billy—the Kid."

But this has never been substantiated.

Hanging around with a rough element in frontier saloons made it almost inevitable that the boy would sooner or later get into some kind of scrape.

He was nearly sixteen when an incident occurred that changed his course of life. An acquaintance of his, a town bum with the picturesque name of "Sombrero Jack," came to him one day in a state of agitation and asked for Billy's help.

Jack had stolen some clothes from the laundry shop of Charley Sun and Sam Chung. They had noticed the loss and raised a great hue and cry about it, and now Jack was afraid to don his new duds and appear in public. Would Billy hide the clothes for him until the trouble blew over?

It didn't seem like much of a crime to Billy, and as Jack was a friend of his, he agreed to do it. He was living at that time in the house of a woman known as the Widow Brown, and he hid the bundle of clothes in her woodshed. Unfortunately the widow found out about the pilferage and she informed Sheriff Whitehall.

The sheriff knew that Billy was a wild boy but not a bad one, and he decided to throw a scare into him to teach him a lesson. More as a joke than anything else, he hauled the frightened boy to the justice of the peace. Justice Givens, however, saw nothing funny in the affair. In his book a crime was a crime no matter how minor it might be. He sent the boy to the town jail to await the action of the grand jury.

It was a deplorable situation for a fifteen-year-old boy. The dismal little adobe jail was an awful place. Other than having boyishly romantic ideas about becoming a cowboy or a gambler Billy really didn't know what he wanted to be in life, but one thing he did know—he didn't want to start out as a prison convict. A few days in the Silver City jailhouse taught him that much.

There was a fireplace in his cell, and though a fullgrown man never could have made it, Billy was a small fifteen. He skinned up through the chimney at night and made his escape in the dark.

This was the beginning—not of a life of crime, but of a brief and tragic life of desperate adventure that would make the youth the most controversial figure in western history. Henry McCarty, alias Billy the Kid, had less than six years left to live. He made the most of them.

Chapter 1

A few hours before sunup Billy slipped into the hotel where he had worked for a while after his mother's death. The Truesdells, man and wife, ran this establishment and they had always had a great liking for the motherless boy. Mr. Truesdell frequently said that Henry McCarty was the only boy who ever worked for him who didn't steal everything that wasn't nailed down.

Billy told them what had happened and that he intended to light out. They thought it was the best thing he could do under the circumstances, and Mrs. Truesdell gave him a square meal and her spare household change. An hour later the boy got on a buckboard that was hauling west for the stage station at the Knight ranch.

The Knight spread was near the Arizona-New Mexico border, and Knight himself had at one time employed Billy's stepfather in his butcher shop in Silver City. He willingly took the boy into his home, but young Billy was apprehensive about remaining in New Mexico.

It didn't seem to him that his so-called crime had

been very earthshaking, but old Justice Givens had said something about him being an "accessory of a felony" —whatever that meant—and he was eager to shake the territorial dust off his heels. Within a few days he was on the trail again. He drifted across the border into Arizona and started west along the Gila River.

It was at this point that the star-crossed boy completely vanished from the sight of recorded history for nearly two years; a circumstance which later gave the legend workers a grand opportunity to compound the mythical Billy the Kid. There is an old saying that if you sling enough mud on a man some of it will stick; in Billy's case nearly all of it has stuck and he seems doomed to wear it through all eternity.

The myth weavers would have it that Billy (just turning sixteen) now proceeded to conduct a one-man reign of terror throughout the length and breadth of Arizona and parts of Old Mexico . . .

They say he bushwhacked three Indians in the Chiricahui Mountains; toppled them off their ponies with three rapid shots.

They say that every time he walked away from a card table he left a dead man behind.

They say he shot down a Negro trooper at Fort Union simply because he didn't like soldiers.

They say he held up prosperous Mexicans in Chihuahua and drilled them if they didn't come across with their money, and that he robbed stagecoaches and rustled great herds of cattle, and they even had him save a party of emigrants from the Apaches in the San Andres Mountains—single-handedly taking on the entire war party and killing eight (some say fourteen!) painted braves.

This brow-raising trail of bloodshed and violent action draws on and on into the realm of incredibility, and it is all pure fabrication. He did not kill a

Negro soldier or any soldier, nor did he ever shoot a fellow gambler over a game of cards. There is absolutely no record that he ever in his life harmed a Mexican or fought with an Indian. Yet to this very day writers persist in repeating the absurd old Upson statement that Billy the Kid killed "twenty-one men, not counting Mexicans and Indians."

Though there are no authentic sources to show how he actually spent those two blank years, it is more than likely that they were relatively uneventful.

What probably happened would have been quite natural for a youth in his particular situation. He rode what was called the "grub line" —herding cattle, branding steers, mending fence, and tracking down rogue lobos; and trying his hand at monte in the various mining camps between jobs. Anything that offered enough hard cash to drift on when the mood hit him. In short, he lived the usual pseudoromantic life of a wandering wrangler.

He drifted back into history in the summer of 1877. The place was Camp Grant, Arizona.

He plodded into town on a weary old pinto who had seen better days. Nobody paid any particular attention to his arrival. As far as they were concerned he was just another saddle tramp.

Billy the Kid did not look like the typical raw-boned, tall-in-the-saddle, iron-eyed gunslinger of early western romance. At seventeen he had reached his full growth, barely standing five feet eight inches high and weighing only a trifle over 130 pounds. His wiry body had a peculiar elasticity which made him quick on his feet and gave him excellent coordination, and his bred-in-the-bone endurance seemed to make him immune to the brutal climate of the plains.

His upper teeth were slightly prominent but not to

13

the point of being "bucked." They gave his tan grey-eyed face the aspect of perpetually wearing a half grin, which came natural to him. He was a good-natured, carefree, rather compassionate boy who believed in letting tomorrow take care of itself. His enemies later said that his eyes were as "cold and deadly" as a rattler's, but his friends always maintained he had "laughing eyes." He had extremely slender hands.

Camp Grant was a ramshackle frontier settlement which served as a stopover for all those restless men of that randy period who wanted to escape from the world of civilized people. Billy's appetite for this kind of adventurous life was whetted by the stirring events of the times and he just naturally rotated toward the gambling dens.

Having some loose cash in his poke he began to frequent the Adkin saloon, trying his luck at monte. Unfortunately there was a certain blowhard blacksmith known as Windy Cahill who also spent a great deal of time in this particular saloon. It would seem there is always a Windy Cahill in any barroom—a big breezy boisterous man who invariably becomes an annoying bully after a few drinks. But Cahill proved to be more than an annoyance to young Billy. He soon became a physical threat.

Time and again he would barge into the saloon like a rambunctious bull in a china shop. In his bellowing way he would make a sudden grab for Billy and start a mock wrestling match. Some match! Windy was twice Billy's age and double his weight and strength. He would slam the boy to the floor, pounce on him and begin to maul him like a playful bear.

Billy repeatedly warned the beefy blacksmith to cut it out and leave him alone, but Cahill would only laugh drunkenly and slap him around some more. The intolerable situation came to a violent head on August 17, 1877.

Cahill, half drunk as usual, threw the helpless boy to the floor, straddled him, and began to slam his head from side to side. At first Billy thought the fool was merely playing his daily role of the great muscle man.

"Let me up," he said. "You're hurting me."

"I want to hurt you," Windy sneered. "That's why I got you down!" He started to bang the boy's head on the floor.

Realizing that he was in the clutches of an enraged brute and suddenly fearing for his life, Billy began to grapple with the big blacksmith. But it was like a midget trying to fight a gorilla. He couldn't budge the huge man. All at once his left hand came into contact with the butt of Cahill's holstered .45 and he snatched out the pistol to use it as a club.

Windy made a snatch for the gun, and during the ensuing struggle for possession of the weapon, it suddenly went off with a deafening roar. The blacksmith jacked straight up, his eyes bugging with stunned bewilderment, and then tipped over on his side.

Billy squirmed free and stood up with the smoking pistol in his hand. The shocked witnesses gawked at him. Cahill was dying and Billy had shot him. As wild and woolly as the West was it still had its laws and no man was totally exempt from them. A killing, no matter how justified, was too often and too quickly settled at the end of a rope.

Billy backed out of the silent saloon and spotted a saddled horse at the hitching rail. He vaulted into the saddle and took off for the New Mexico line. That was his first killing and, contrary to popular belief, very few were slated to follow it.

He reached Knight's ranch that night, explained what had happened, asked for the loan of another horse, and asked Knight if he would see that the "borrowed" horse, Cashaw, was returned to its owner in Camp Grant. This was typical of Billy; he always settled his debts. Horse thieving was the ultimate crime in the West and he didn't want it on his record.

He didn't waste any time at Knight's ranch. As soon as he had another pony and a grubstake in his saddlebag he headed into the Burro Mountains of southwestern New Mexico, with the intention of losing himself among the isolated mining camps that dotted that barren region.

It was while killing time in one of those back-trail camps that he picked up a hand-me-down copy of the Arizona *Citizen*, dated August 22, 1877, and saw his name in print for the first time.

The article said that E.P.Cahill had been shot and killed in Camp Grant, and the coroner's jury had found that the shooting "was criminal and unjustifiable, and that Henry Antrim, alias Kid is guilty thereof." The names of the carefully selected coroner's jury were given and Billy knew every one of them. They had all been friends of Windy Cahill's.

So much for his chances of receiving a fair trial in Arizona!

The newspaper made him cognizant of a new danger. Too many people in the Burro camps knew he was Henry Antrim and some of them had probably read this very article. One of them just might attempt to turn him in to the law on the off chance of collecting a reward. So—it was time to ramble again.

It was also time to do something about his name. Using it was like wearing a Wanted for Murder poster. Now that he was on the dodge he would have to pick an alias . . . .Lots of people had called him Billy, after his stepfather, so why not substitute William H. for Henry? He would have to drop the Antrim and McCarty too, not only for his own sake but in order to keep the stigma of disgrace from his family.

He selected "Bonney" out of the air. William H. Bonney. It sounded good. It was a name which stuck with a vengeance. He had no idea how completely lost Henry McCarty and Henry Antrim were destined to become, or how much research grief this pseudonym would cause future scholars and historians.

Haunted by the article he had read, Billy lost no time in saddling up and making tracks. He was already beginning to imagine that some of the camp loafers were looking at him with dollar-sign eyes.

He rode out of camp casually, like a man going nowhere in particular, down out of the foothills and into the desert night. After a mile he turned off the road. It had been fairly straight on the flat and he took a line on a star. A couple of miles north he turned east again, holding the star ahead of him. He maintained an easy lope and every so often he stopped to listen. The star-shot mesa was incredibly still.

He found a trail leading southeast and he paralleled it. Some miles on ahead he could see the line of the mesa top. In the canyons of the broken wall of the tableland was where some of the local ranchers homesteaded precious water. It seemed like a good place for him to lay low for a while.

In the morning he rode across a canyon mouth and picked up a stream and followed it down the arroyo. Water from the stream had pooled in a sunny pond, and beyond the land rose in broken timbered folds. It was like an oasis—but it was already occupied. Four or five riders had set up camp by the pond.

It was an uneasy moment for all of them. The law was after Billy for murder, and a posse was after the riders for horse stealing. But they soon learned that they were all in the same boat and they settled down to make friends.

Jesse Evans, a young cowboy gone bad, was the leader of the gang. There is a persistent legend that Jesse and Billy had been boyhood chums back in Silver City, and perhaps it is true. If it is, then Jesse certainly knew that Billy was Henry Antrim.

At any rate Jesse seemed to take a great liking to young Billy, and he boasted how he and his pals had been kicking up a little trouble in the Burros. For a lark they had stolen three ponies from the Pass coal camp and now a posse was looking for them.

He also told Billy that they were from the Pecos country in Lincoln County where, he said, a slam-bang range war was getting ready to erupt. No end of gunslingers, thieves and rustlers had been drifting into the county lately because Lincoln was the perfect hideout for outlaws—especially, he explained, if you worked for the right people, as Jesse and his pals did.

Billy was led to understand that by the "right people" Jesse meant an outfit known as the Murphy-Dolan firm in the town of Lincoln. It seemed that Murphy &Co. owned the county sheriff.

"You ride for Jimmy Dolan," Jesse said, "and you got no trouble with law, no matter what you might have done."

It sounded all right, but Billy wasn't overly impressed by Jesse and his boys. They liked to pass themselves off as carefree rowdies out to have a wild time, but underneath their veneer of good-natured "fun" ran an obvious streak of downright meanness. They were the sort who would deliberately create a ruckus for the opportunity to settle it with their six-shooters.

Legend has it that Frank Baker and Bill Morton were two of the boys who were in the arroyo camp that day, and that they didn't take to Billy the way

18

Jesse did. In any event Billy decided to remain on his own. He wasn't looking for any more trouble than he already had. He saddled up, intending to head southeast to the little town of Mesilla. Jesse said they would ride along with him as far as the Rio Grande, and Billy knew better than to object.

With the three stolen horses in tow, the little band rode down the arroyo and started for Cooks Canyon. Out beyond the broken, spurred edge of the canyon, the mesa began to take shape against the stainless dazzle of sky. Billy was wondering how he could shake his new *compadres* without hurting their peppery feelings.

Suddenly they heard galloping hoofs, one rider, on the road ahead. In the next moment the rider appeared in the mouth of the canyon and reined in when he saw Jesse's gang. Billy recognized him as a man he had met in one of the mining camps.

Assuming that Jesse's banditti would likely start a fight, Billy quietly turned his pony off to one side and followed the precipitous wall of the escarpment along a rising path. Gaining the top of the ridge he halted and looked back. A big dust cloud boiled out of the plain below, made by Jesse and his boys. There hadn't been any trouble after all.

Billy put his pony over the rocky brow and moseyed toward the Rio Grande. He didn't know it then, but that chance meeting with the lone rider in the canyon was to have a drastic effect on his short life.

Chapter 2

Mesilla was a small, lazy town with many sun-scorched plazas and not too many *gringos* (Anglo-Americans). Billy liked it and the Mexican inhabitants liked him. He talked their lingo and he knew how to lead their kind of life; an easygoing day-to-day existence that placed great trust in *mañana*.

He loafed around in the plazas, played a little monte in the cantinas, and wasn't in any hurry to make up his mind as to where he should go or what he should do next. *Mañana* was always soon enough. But this idyllic life ended abruptly when he happened to notice an article in the Mesilla Valley *Independent*. Again his name leaped out at him in boldface print:

"On Monday last, three horses . . .were stolen from Pass coal camp in the Burro Mountains . . . Sometime on Tuesday the party of thieves, among whom were Henry Antrim, were met at Cooks Canyon by Mr. Carpenter. Telegrams have been sent to Sheriff Barela at Mesilla, and we hope to hear of the arrest of the thieves . . ."

Not so good. That lone rider, Carpenter, had recognized him among the banditti. Now the local sheriff was probably prowling around looking for him at that very moment. If he was nabbed by the law for horse stealing he would in all likelihood be extradited back to Arizona to stand trial for the Cahill shooting—which would mean a very short ride on a noose.

Funny how his luck seemed to go sour on him time and again. He hid some clothes to help a friend and was thrown in jail. He accidentally shot a man in self-defense and he is charged with murder. He ran into some rustlers and was labeled a horsethief. But the milk was spilt now and he wasn't the type to cry over it. He would have to hit the trail again—the sooner the better.

Gathering up his gear took no time at all. Like any western drifter, he always traveled light. A pony, a saddle, saddlebags, bedroll, an old Colt and a cheap Winchester were his total belongings. With these few possessions he furnished his enormous house. The mesas were his floors, the mountains his walls, and the sky was his roof. He always felt perfectly at home.

The best plan he could think of at the moment was to take up Jesse Evans on his offer. He would go to Lincoln County, get a job riding for this Jimmy Dolan, and lay low. If trouble came to Lincoln, as Jesse had prophesied, he could always clear out. But there wasn't any sense in stewing over it now. Wait till it happened, then see. He didn't believe in borrowing trouble.

He crossed the Rio Grande at Las Cruces and followed the trail up into the San Andres Mountains, reaching the San Agustin Pass before twilight. He gave his lathered nag a breather and sat relaxed in the saddle, gazing down at the beautiful panoramic scene of the Tularosa Valley.

The barren, townless region of White Sands was

directly below him, and far off in the east the granite heights of the Sacramento Mountains hulked into the crepuscular sky with a brooding godlike intensity, all red and blue and purple and ribbed with deep secret canyons. And still farther east rose the castle crags and turret peaks of El Capitan. That was his landmark. Lincoln was situated on the Rio Bonito where it snaked through Bonito Canyon just west of the looming Capitans.

He started across White Sands as the dusk of the desert basin deepened and the signal peaks of the Andres began shooting out lingering sparks with the red fire of sunset. In the hushed gloom of the desert, with the vast herd of enduring stars spanned over his head, Billy the Kid slowly rode toward his rendezvous with destiny.

There are moments in our history when it seems as though fate deliberately arranged matters for the express purpose of allowing certain preselected mortals to achieve lasting fame. Billy the Kid could not have chosen a more auspicious time to arrive in Lincoln County. A bitter feud was definitely in the making.

The causes of the Lincoln County War were so complex and far-reaching that today many facets of the feud have become totally obscured. In essence the situation was this. New Mexico was a territory, not a state, and it was dominated by a group of powerful politicians known as the Santa Fe Ring.

These gentlemen controlled the law, the tax collectors, and most of the government contracts and mercantile trade. In short, they milked the Territory for all it was worth. Lincoln was the largest county in New Mexico and it was lush pickings for the Ring.

Major L.G. Murphy, a grizzled old ex-army officer, was the Ring's representative in the town of Lincoln. He and a tough thirty-year-old Irishman named Jimmy Dolan ran a mercantile house which dealt in everything from rotgut whiskey to rustled cattle. Murphy made the mistake of drinking too much of his own whiskey, thus becoming permanently insensible, and Dolan took over the management of "The House." He had a junior partner, one John Riley.

The most profitable business in New Mexico at that time was in government contracts which supplied the army posts and Indian reservations with beef. In order to fill these contracts Dolan hired a raft of minor desperadoes to rustle the required cattle.

To men like Jesse Evans, Frank Baker, and Bill Morton the most obvious place to find free beef-on-the-hoof was on John Chisum's vast range, which sprawled along the Pecos River. Chisum was the biggest cattleman in the world, holding more than 60,000 longhorns at a time on his grazing land.

Chisum naturally resented this "moonlighting" on his herd, and in retaliation he talked a thirty-two-year-old lawyer by the name of Alexander McSween to come to Lincoln and open a mercantile house in competition with Murphy & Co.

John Tunstall, a twenty-six-year-old English gentleman, was McSween's partner in this venture and most of the business was put in his name. Their purpose was to undersell Murphy & Co., to gain the goodwill of the small ranchers in the county by opening a bank to accommodate their needs, and to establish a cow camp on the Rio Feliz.

Murphy & Co. suffered an immediate business slump and were embittered by this sudden intrusion on their fat profits. More than that—what affected Murphy & Co. also affected the Santa Fe Ring, and they began to pressure Jimmy Dolan to break up the McSween-Tunstall combine before it was too late. Dolan, a mean fighter, was more than willing to do his best. He began to cast about for gunslingers.

So war clouds gathered over Lincoln County; dark angry banks rising and preparing to clash together with a roar of thunder. The Murphy-Dolan-Riley faction with hired gunmen and the machinery of the law on one side, and the Chisum-McSween-Tunstall faction with a handful of small ranchers on the other. The balance of power definitely rested with Murphy & Co.

To further complicate matters, Murphy once had a partner named Emil Fritz who had gone to Germany on a visit and had died there, leaving a will and an insurance policy valued at $10,000. Fritz' brother and sister were the beneficiaries, and fearing that Murphy would find some legal loophole to swindle them out of their inheritance, they hired McSween to collect on the policy.

McSween went to New York and managed to get possession of the money, but to do so cost him well over $3,000, which he deducted from the $10,000. On his return to Lincoln he discovered that Murphy had started a legal hassle with Fritz' beneficiaries, so he banked the remainder of the insurance money in his own name and simply sat pat to wait and see what would develop.

This contested insurance money was the spark that finally ignited the Lincoln County War, claimed the lives of over thirty men, and made Billy the Kid immortal.

Billy rode with spurs a-jingle into the town of Lincoln and eased his pony to a walk. The dust in the street was near to ankle deep on his horse. Other horses, some saddled with riders, some drawing rattly buckboards, were kicking up dust that rolled and drifted like yellow smoke.

The town was just one long dirt street with maybe twenty buildings, large and small, stretched out along either side of it. Stockton's saloon, the jail and courthouse, a couple of corrals, Tunstall's store next to McSween's house, the Wortley Hotel across the street from Murphy & Co . . .almost all one-story adobe, though here and there a second story of flimsy unpainted pine had been added. None of the buildings touched; each stood in its own isolated little kingdom of weed and dirt.

Behind the north side of the town the sunbaked earth sloped down to a river bed where the Rio Bonito sang among the willows. Steep piñon-stippled hills rolled up on either side of the somnolent village. But it wasn't all sleepy. As Billy moseyed by the Murphy store, an old two-story adobe with a small upstairs porch in front, a couple of men stepped out and gave him a truculent stare. One of them wore a badge.

Billy turned out of town. His pony clop-clopped down the winding powdery road, and then the canyon opened up and showed him a pleasant vega of Mexican farmlands, oak-brush hills, agricultural valleys and lofty plateaus. He followed the Bonito down to where it joined the Rio Ruidoso and they both became the Rio Hondo, flowing east to the Pecos River.

He spent the next two weeks riding the grub line, picking up random jobs branding and herding with the small outfits in the fertile Pecos region. He talked with the ranchers and other riders and was able to form a fairly composite picture of the uneasy situation that existed in the county. Most of the small ranchers had been in hock up to their ears with Murphy & Co. for years, and now Jimmy Dolan was putting the squeeze on them with the intention of forcing them into bankruptcy and off their land.

Prior to the advent of the McSween-Tunstall store and bank, Murphy and Dolan had held the monopoly of the sale of all merchandise in Lincoln and the little cattlemen and farmers had had no option but to deal with them; which had been tantamount to selling their souls to the devil. McSween had recently made a written report regarding the usurious methods employed by Murphy & Co:

The farmers would buy merchandise from them at exorbitant prices and were compelled to turn in their produce in payment thereof at prices that suited Murphy & Co., and if a farmer refused to do so, he was subjected to intimidation and the whole judicial machinery (meaning Sheriff Brady who was on Murphy's payroll) was used to accomplish that object. The result was that Murphy & Co. were absolute monarchs of Lincoln County and ruled their subjects with an oppressive iron heel.

It didn't sound good to Billy. Being an underdog himself, he invariably took the side of other little men who were in the same fix. The idea that a mercantile house could use the law as a means to increase its own illegal gains was downright medieval.

What really rubbed him wrong was that Murphy and Dolan, in their deliberate attempt to break the Chisum-McSween-Tunstall combine, were squeezing dry the multitude of helpless Mexican farmers who were trying to eke a living out of the harsh land. These people were the only true friends the seventeen-year-old boy had ever known. He thought of them as *los pobres*, the poor ones; they called him *el Cabrito*, the Kid.

On the other hand he had met John Chisum on one of his rambles across the Pecos and he had not been favorably impressed by the sturdy fifty-six-year-old frontiersman who had carved a cattle empire out of an Apache-ridden wilderness. Old "Uncle John" seemed to be far more interested in looking out for his own vast holdings than in trying to right any wrongs. He had no more compassion for the lowly *pobres* than drunken old Murphy had.

Billy drifted south along the Pecos, looking, listening, trying to make up his mind which way he should jump if the percolating situation in Lincoln suddenly boiled into war. Somewhere below the Rio Penasco he found one of Murphy & Co's old corrals. Jesse Evans and a few of his rowdies were camped there.

Jesse was delighted to see him again, thinking that Billy had decided to join up with the Murphy-Dolan faction. The excitement, he told his young friend, was ready to pop any time now. Colonel W. L. Rynerson, the District Prosecuting Attorney and a big wheel in the Santa Fe Ring, had urged Dolan to smash the Chisum-McSween-Tunstall faction at any cost.

It seemed pretty obvious to Billy that the deck was being heavily stacked against the weaker party. He asked Jesse what he knew about Chisum's two partners McSween and Tunstall.

Jesse hated them, especially Alexander McSween; a Bible-pounding, psalm-singing, goody-goody man, he said disgustedly. The truth was that Jesse, Frank Baker, Tom Hill, and George Davis had recently been arrested and thrown in the Lincoln calaboose for stealing some of Tunstall's horses, and the lawyer McSween had willingly agreed to prosecute them. Nothing had come of it, however, because Sheriff Brady had "forgotten" to lock the jailhouse door, and Jesse and his boys had made an easy escape. But they would get even, Jesse vowed. They would fix McSween's wagon as soon as Dolan said the word.

John Tunstall, he said contemptuously, was a horse of another color. Jesse and his banditti had never seen his like before. He was an English dude— a city dandy who dressed neatly and talked with a highfalutin accent.

27

"He'll be a pushover for us," was Jesse's way of dismissing the topic. He then asked if Billy was ready to ride for Dolan's outfit, and Billy hedged by replying, "It's possible."

He strongly doubted it. He liked Jesse well enough as a campfire *compadre* but he didn't much care to ride with him in a range war. Jesse Evans was a true western badman. Billy the Kid was not. But just to round out his information and get himself thoroughly oriented, he saddled up to go have a looksee at Dolan's cow camp across the Pecos. He and Jesse shook goodby, and Billy clucked at his pony.

It would be a long time before the two young riders met again on friendly terms.

Billy forded the Pecos near Seven Rivers, where various tributaries join the parent river to form a candelabra pattern on New Mexico maps, and rode into Dolan's sprawling cow camp. Bill Morton had been elevated to the position of "ramrod" for Dolan's outfit since Billy had last seen him in Cooks Canyon.

Morton was a young, tough, hardheaded Virginian with better than average intelligence and a great deal of personal courage. He and Billy had not hit it off in the Burro Mountains and their natural emnity was even more pronounced on this second meeting.

Jimmy Dolan, the fiery boy-faced boss, had heard of Kid Antrim from Jesse Evans and he was eager to hire him as a gunhand-rider. But Morton thought otherwise. Possibly he noticed Billy's reluctance about a proposal to rustle some of Tunstall's cattle which were grazing north of Seven Rivers. At any rate he and Billy got into a violent altercation on the second day and Billy set himself to make a quick hook and draw with his secondhand Colt.

It did not come to gunplay. At that time few of the wranglers in Dolan's camp had ever been in an actual gunfight, and they all knew that this boy who called himself Billy Bonney had killed a man in Arizona and none of them were eager to try him. This was not the Hollywood West of the legendary and overly exaggerated Showdown. Relatively few men of the Real West were inclined to risk their lives at pistol-point for the sake of a mere argument.

It was because of such minor incidents as this that Billy the Kid's reputation as a "smiling killer" began to spread in the Southwest—a reputation which he never made any attempt to live up to; on the contrary he did his level best to live it down, but neither the law nor the legends that haunted him gave him a chance to succeed.

Backing away from Morton's bunch, Billy mounted his pony and pointed for the Hondo. This was the final decision which settled his fate. He definitely would not throw in with Dolan's crowd. The die was cast. He rode into the westering sun. The Lincoln County War—only ten weeks off—lay waiting for him across the river like an unseen deadfall.

He had just turned eighteen.

Chapter 3

It was early winter, 1877, and an ear-chilling wind came crisply across the mesa and robbed the creek-held willows of their greenery. George Coe, a Mc-Sween-Tunstall supporter, had a small ranch near the joint of the Ruidoso and Bonito only ten miles south of Lincoln, and Billy made a stopover there which turned into a one-month stay.

He and George Coe got on well, filling out the winter days with the usual ranch chores, hunting deer and wild turkey, and spending the nights before a crackling fire with a bottle of wine and a guitar. Maybe one night a week they would attend a Mexican dance at nearby San Patricio, where Billy was a great favorite among the black-eyed Mexican belles.

During this lackadaisical period Billy met George's cousin, Frank Coe, and three firebrand ranchers named Doc Scurlock, Charlie Bowdre, and Frank McNab; also a levelheaded young rancher named Dick Brewer who had all the instincts of a natural leader. All of these men were anti-Murphy & Co. Brewer was the foreman of Tunstall's ranch on the Rio Feliz, and he arranged a meeting of the young drifter and the young Englishman.

Tunstall was a handsome, well-educated aristocrat who had recently arrived in America to seek his fortune in the Southwest. Impeccable in manner, speech and dress, he and the poorly-educated cowboy made an incongruous pair. Yet for some strange reason Billy and Tunstall got on like a pair of devoted brothers.

Billy was frankly awed by Tunstall's innate courtesy, compassion and brilliance. He had never seen a real gentleman before and he was totally enchanted by this gracious Englishman. Having been reared among dance-hall girls, tinhorn gamblers, gunmen, rustlers, miners and no end of saddle tramps, Tunstall must have appeared in his impressionable young mind as an almost Christlike figure. He idolized the man.

On his side, Tunstall was amazed that a lawless frontier could produce a parentless, outlawed boy who was capable of so much understanding and sensitivity. He quickly saw that Billy, in spite of a greatly handicapped education, had an excellent mind and a deep desire to learn. He seemed to have no aspirations toward fame and fortune; he simply wanted to be accepted among the world's men of goodwill.

It was an odd friendship—breeding and culture mingling with ignorance and outlawry—and it ripened into an alliance that was akin to a blood pact. Billy went to work for Tunstall at the first of the new year, riding the fifty-mile trail between the Englishman's Rio Feliz ranch and his store in Lincoln.

Tunstall gave his young rider a new horse and saddle and a Colt pistol, and Billy choked up and had to turn away quickly. When Frank Coe asked him what was the matter, the boy said:

"It's the first time in my life anybody ever gave

me anything."

He named his new pony Old Grey.

It was while making his weekly jaunt into Lincoln that Billy met Tunstall's partner, the enigmatic Alexander McSween. Billy got on well with McSween's vivacious young wife Susan, who had all the strength and determination of a typical pioneer woman, but not so well with McSween himself.

To Billy's mind Jesse Evans had been right: the lawyer was a Bible-pounding idealist who spouted meaningless psalms as easily as a mule-driver could cuss a balky team. McSween was a pacifist, a man who thought the West could be tamed with legal verbosity instead of six-gun violence. But Billy, who had been reared on the brawling frontier, knew better. First came Colt law—then judicial law could follow.

The eighteen-year-old drifter and the thirty-two year old lawyer held some heated discussions over this controversy and, ironically, each was destined to die according to his own beliefs: the one empty-handed, the other armed for defense.

It was at this time that Billy read a startling article in an issue of the Mesilla *Independent*, dated January 26, 1878. The item had been written by Tunstall and concerned the county taxes that had been collected by Sheriff Brady. According to the article the McSween-Tunstall establishment had given the sheriff a $1,500 check for Territorial taxes and Brady had proceeded to sign the check over to John Riley, who in turn had used it to pay off some of The House's cattle debts. Murphy & Co. were paying their bills with county tax money given to them by the sheriff!

McSween and Tunstall had the canceled check to prove their story. The back of the check had been endorsed by William Brady and John Riley. The article ended by saying: "A delinquent tax payer is bad; a delinquent tax collector is worse."

This really kicked a hole in the hornet's nest. The Santa Fe Ring was outraged that Murphy & Co. could pull such a stupid blunder *and* get caught at it! Old Major Murphy was too befuddled by booze to know what it was all about, but Jimmy Dolan knew that something had to be done before the game was lost. He hurriedly adopted an old military maxim: If the enemy attacks your front, counterattack his flank.

Mr. and Mrs. McSween had recently departed for Las Vegas to join Chisum at a business conference in the East, and this gave Dolan the opportunity he was looking for to make his counterattack. He took the first stage to Mesilla, which was the seat of the District Court, and paid a visit to the sister of the deceased Emil Fritz.

Had McSween, he asked, given her the money on her brother's insurance policy yet? No, he hadn't. Well, did she know that McSween had banked her money under his name? No, she hadn't known that. Well, did she know that McSween and his wife had recently left Lincoln to go to Las Vegas, and then on to St. Louis? No, she hadn't known that either. Well then, Dolan shrewdly suggested, didn't it look as if McSween intended to run out with her money?

Seeing that he had the poor woman flustered with concern, he quickly pressed home his point. The only way she could protect herself and her money, he told her, was to charge McSween with embezzlement. All she had to do was say the word and Dolan would handle the arrangements.

Fritz' sister didn't want to cause any trouble, but she did want her money. She certainly had no idea that her decision would trigger the Lincoln County War. She said all right.

Dolan worked the indictment through Tom Catron who was the chief lawyer of the Santa Fe Ring.

A warrant for McSween was sworn out in Mesilla and forwarded to Las Vegas. At the same time Mc-Sween was arrested Catron also managed to have John Chisum arrested, purely on a technicality.

Shrewd old Uncle John must have suspected that this was the beginning of a shooting war and he wisely decided to sit it out. He let himself be locked up in the Las Vegas jail and made no plea for bail, leaving McSween and Tunstall to handle the hot potato.

McSween, outraged at being trapped by a legal trick, elected to fight back. He demanded to be set free on bail until the time of his trial which was scheduled for April of that year. But to apply for bail he would have to go to Mesilla. In the custody of Deputy Sheriff Barrier of Las Vegas, McSween started the long journey back to Lincoln.

The Murphy-Dolan faction was delighted by the catastrophe that had struck their enemies a double blow. Chisum in jail and McSween hamstrung by a deputy guard! Now all they had to do was to fix that dude Englishman, and then they would have complete control of the county again and could get on with the shearing of the golden fleece.

Tunstall, Billy, and Dick Brewer were waiting in Lincoln when McSween arrived with his keeper, Deputy Barrier. They all went into the lawyer's ten-room adobe home to discuss this unexpected disaster. There was no way of getting around it: either McSween made the 150 mile ride to Mesilla to effect his release on bail, or Deputy Barrier would have to lock him up in the nearest jail and keep him there. Barrier was sorry but he had his orders.

So be it. Tunstall said he would go to Mesilla with his partner.

This proposal sounded chancy to Billy and he offered to accompany his boss, just in case. But Tunstall laughed at his fears. Nothing could happen to them as long as they were in Barrier's custody. Like McSween, the Englishman was innocently willing to put his trust in the law. Billy, however, knew how easily frontier law could be twisted into a treacherous weapon, but he couldn't make Tunstall see it.

McSween, Tunstall, and Barrier set out for Mesilla the following day. Billy and Brewer immediately rode toward the Honda to look for allies among the small ranchers. From all indications they were soon going to need all the support they could scare up.

In Mesilla the Santa Fe Ring cracked down on McSween with all its judicial might. With the help of Judge Bristol, Prosecuting Attorney Rynerson had the bail set at $30,000! McSween of course did not have access to any such exorbitant sum, so the court issued writs of attachment against all of his property in Lincoln. It was a brutal blow, but at least McSween was now out on bail. He, Tunstall, and Barrier started back to Lincoln on February 5.

That night they made camp at the foot of San Agustin Pass. Seemingly out of nowhere Jimmy Dolan, Jesse Evans, Frank Baker, Tom Hill, and George Davis suddenly strode up to the fire. Dolan's intentions were as obvious as the carbine he held in his hands. He insulted Tunstall with vile language, doing his best to egg the Englishman into a fight.

Tunstall merely smiled and shook his head, refusing to be provoked into sudden death. Deputy Barrier, with the weight of the law behind him, intervened and told Dolan and his hired gunhands to clear out. The hassle lasted only a few minutes, and then the belligerents backed off and vanished in the dark.

Dolan rode homeward in a happy frame of mind. He had just picked up a useful bit of information. Writs of attachment had been issued against McSween's property. Good! He would see that his pal

35

Sheriff Brady put the writs into effect . . .but not quite in the manner the law expected.

It was Saturday when Billy rode into Lincoln with two stanch Tunstall supporters: Bob Widenmann, a US deputy marshal, and Fred Waite, a quarter-breed Cherokee. The town was in a hurly-burly. A number of Dolan's riders were raucously roving the long street and more were racking in from either end of town. As soon as the three Tunstall men dismounted Dolan's crowd belligerently gathered around them, and it was probably only the fact that Widenmann was carrying a marshal's commission that held them in check.

That great upholder of law and order Sheriff Brady was swaggering around Tunstall's store slapping attachment notices on the doors. He had already attached everything McSween owned.

"You have no right to attach this store," Widenmann said angrily. "It's in Tunstall's name. The writs only concern McSween."

All of which meant absolutely nothing to Brady. Dolan had given him his orders and he intended to carry them out. He knew on which side his bread was buttered. He had deputized five of Dolan's men and he now posted them inside the store. That was that.

There was nothing Billy and his two *compadres* could do about this travesty of justice. They were outnumbered six to one, and Dolan's gang was looking for an excuse to start a fight. Bill Morton was there and he would have liked nothing better than the chance to turn Billy the Kid into a bloody sieve.

McSween and Tunstall arrived at noon and the young Englishman was furious when he learned what Brady had done. The sheriff turned a deaf ear on his protests, maintaining that his behavior was justified inasmuch as McSween and Tunstall were business partners. Meanwhile still more riders were clattering into town, and Billy, Waite, and Widenmann finally went over to their horses to draw their rifles.

Tunstall, realizing that they were teetering on the verge of a gun brawl, gave up his fruitless argument with Brady and asked if he could at least be allowed to send his own riding mounts out of town. He kept nine of them in the corral behind his store.

Bighearted Brady said yes, he would exempt the horses from his attachment. Tunstall told his men to put away their rifles and get the horses out of Lincoln before the sheriff changed his mind. Actually, Brady was playing it cagey. He intended to wait until Tunstall had collected all his livestock at his ranch—then he would slap a blanket attachment on the whole kit and caboodle.

It was illegal as sin, but Brady was the law in Lincoln County and Tunstall had been brought up to abide by the law, right or wrong. Billy didn't see it that way. Docilely riding along with corrupt legislation in the West too often rode you smack into the gallows. He urged Tunstall to call in his allies and fight. The time for armed resistance was now.

No; Tunstall did not agree. Violence never proved anything. They would have to fight their battle in a court of law, not in the street or on the range. He told the three men to take his exempted horses to Dick Brewer's place for the night; then herd them on down to the Rio Feliz ranch the next day.

On February 12 Brady was ready to take his next giant step. He deputized Jacob "Billy" Mathews and gave him a posse of twenty-some Dolan men, ordering him to go serve an attachment notice on Tunstall's ranch. Joggling out of town on their ponies the armed band had all the earmarks of a war party, and many of the apprehensive civilians who watched them go began to think it might be a good time to move out of Lincoln.

Mathews' posse ran into an obstinate snag on the 13th. In Tunstall's absence, Dick Brewer was in command of the Rio Feliz ranch and he, Billy Bonney, Bob Widenmann, Fred Waite, and a rider named John Middleton had barricaded themselves inside the ranch house and were ready and waiting for battle.

Hothead Bill Morton wanted to storm the house, and he urged Mathews to split his force and hit the enemy from two sides. But Mathews hung fire. Brady had told him to serve an attachment notice; he hadn't said anything about starting a range war. He decided not to fight, ordered his posse to pull back to a nearby ranch, and sent Morton posthaste to Lincoln for new orders from Brady and Dolan.

About that same time Tunstall learned what was happening on the Rio Feliz and he set out for the Pecos, hoping to somehow forestall the crisis that was rapidly expanding over the county like a swelling cyclone. His first stop was at Chisum's South Spring ranch, where he hoped to gain support for his faction. But sly old Uncle John was still snug in jail and he had warned his people to stay out of the feud. Somewhat discouraged, Tunstall turned south.

Arriving at his ranch on the 16th he tried to reason with his combat-ready cohorts, stubbornly contending that they could reach a peaceful understanding with Brady and Dolan providing that no one made the fool mistake of resorting to gunplay.

Billy and Brewer disagreed vehemently. It was too late to light the peace pipes, they argued. Dolan was out to break Tunstall and he was wielding Brady and his phony writs like a ball and chain.

"You've *got* to fight," Billy told the pacifist Englishman.

Tunstall refused. He would rather relinquish his property than cause bloodshed. To his gentle nature there was nothing disgraceful about a tactical re-treat. The next day he sent Fred Waite out to inform Mathews that he intended to abandon his ranch and livestock. Mathews and his men could move in on the 18th and serve their writ. Tunstall would leave his German caretaker, "Old Man" Gauss, behind as his representative. He also informed Mathews that he planned to move his nine exempted horses to Brewer's little ranch on the Rio Ruidoso.

Billy was frankly worried about Tunstall's life. He figured that Dolan and Brady didn't really give a hoot about his boss' ranch and stock, they simply wanted Tunstall dead. If the Englishman wouldn't fight, then he should at least try to save his life.

"Forget about your horses," he urged his friend, "and hide out in the hills till we see which way the smoke blows."

Tunstall smilingly refused. Why should he hide in the hills like a common criminal? He had broken no law, there was no warrant out for him. Right up to the very end he did not understand the deadly threat that hovered over him.

Just before dawn on February 18, 1878, Tunstall, Billy, Brewer, Widenmann, and Middleton rode out of the ranch with the nine exempted horses and struck across the rolling grasslands for the Hondo.

At eight a.m. Mathews' posse pulled into the ranch and was greeted by Old Man Gauss who answered all their questions candidly. Godfrey Gauss was from the Old Country and he didn't understand all this Wild West shoot'm-up business. It was no skin off his nose what happened to Tunstall, Brewer, and Bonney.

Perhaps by this time Deputy Mathews had received fresh instructions from Brady and Dolan, or maybe he had made up his own mind as to what should be done next. One way or another he selected a special posse, put Bill Morton in command, and told them to go after Tunstall. He didn't have to tell them anything else. Jesse Evans and his three gun-slingers, Baker, Hill and Davis, were among the thirteen-man posse. They all knew what they were going to do.

Tunstall's boys had made a slow ride of it. It was late afternoon and they were now approaching the timbered foothills south of the Ruidoso. They had nearly reached Brewer's ranch and the somnolent hills with the muted flut-flutter of wild turkeys in the chaparral thickets had lulled them into a false sense of security.

Billy and Middleton were lazing along on the far side of the nine horses. Brewer and Widenmann were parallel to them on the nigh side. Tunstall was riding drag by himself in the rear. Middleton mentioned to Billy that it might be a good idea to knock over a fat tom turkey for dinner that night at Brewer's place. Billy was about to agree when something suddenly went *zzzmmm* between their ponies and kicked up a spout of dirt ahead of them. Then they heard the *ka-pow* of a distant shot.

They pulled up and turned in their saddles. A gang of horsemen was humping over a near hill and riding hell-for-leather straight at them! Billy couldn't be sure if Tunstall, Brewer, and Widenmann had seen Morton's crowd. Yelling, "Warn the boss," at Middleton, he spurred toward his other two *compadres*.

Dick Brewer and Bob Widenmann had not seen the posse. The scrubby little foothills they had just entered lay around them like meatballs on a platter. They saw Billy riding toward them from about 200 yards off, and all at once a great raft of riders cleared the brow of a hill directly behind the Kid and opened fire. Brewer and Widenmann socked in the iron and went tearing for the nearest hill, which was corrugated with tumbled rocks and spiked with oaks.

Meanwhile Middleton, the closest man to Tunstall, yelled, "Look out—posse!" at the Englishman, and then went galloping after Billy. But Tunstall made no attempt toward flight. He halted and dismounted as the posse came charging up. He was still determined to play the pacifist, and he held up his pistol, butt first, to Morton.

Tom Hill didn't give him a chance to surrender. He fired a shot from his saddle and the bullet plowed through the back of Tunstall's head. Another rider (some say Morton, others say Evans) fired a slug into the crumpled Englishman's chest. Hill then turned his smoking gun on Tunstall's horse and shot the poor beast dead.

Legend here rears its bloodthirsty head again and says that one of Morton's men diabolically pounded in Tunstall's face with a jagged rock. But this is not true.

Brewer and Widenmann urged their lathered mounts up the rocky hill, piled out of their saddles and hunkered down in a boulder pile with their Winchesters. Billy came humping up the slope and joined them among the rocks, and a moment later Middleton pounded up with his rifle already in hand. The four men deployed themselves in a small protected perimeter and prepared to make a stand.

"They killed Tunstall," Middleton gasped. "He wouldn't run."

Billy closed his eyes. He had thought that Tunstall was right behind him and Middleton. Why had the courageous fool elected to stay with his horses? The odds were three to one in Morton's favor and any Westerner had the sense to run for cover when the deck was stacked against him.

The posse passed below them, just out of rifle range, and wheeled around the shoulder of a hill. To kill a lone unresisting man was child's play, but to go up against four armed gunfighters was something else. Morton decided to leave Brewer's boys alone.

Jesse Evans and Tom Hill were already beginning to have second thoughts about their rash act. They had not been deputized by Brady or Mathews and it was hard to tell what view the Territorial law would take on the killing. They decided to strike out for Texas. Frank Baker and George Davis elected to stay on in Lincoln and take their chances with Dolan and Brady.

It was dark soon and Brewer and his three friends cleared out for Lincoln. Each had recognized some of the possemen and they compared notes on the names of Tunstall's murderers: Morton, Baker, Evans, Hill, Davis, "Buckshot" Roberts, Wallace Olinger, Bob Beckwith, George Hindman, Pantaleon Gallegos·. . .

Billy had little to say on that somber ride. He was thinking about the men who had murdered his friend. He believed in an eye for an eye.

Chapter 4

Nearly forty McSween-Tunstall partisans gathered in the lawyer's home late that night to listen to the grim tale Dick Brewer had to relate. McSween was heartsick over the loss of his friend, but he admonished his allies against resorting to violence. He, like his dead partner, still believed in the right and might of the law, even when it was in the hands of a hireling such as Brady.

A remarkable thing happened at midnight. John Riley, Dolan's junior partner, stumbled into McSween's house as drunk as a lord! Perhaps in his befuddled condition he had mistaken the private residence for the town saloon. Whatever the reason, he was suddenly there and it was a mighty dangerous spot for a man in his position. Billy and some of the other furious men wanted to drop him where he stood, but Riley had enough sense left to quickly surrender his pistol. Billy told him to keep digging—empty his pockets on the table.

Among the articles that Riley had to shell out was a small notebook which listed the names of all the rustlers Dolan had hired. It showed exactly how much each moonlight cowboy had coming to him from The House at $5 per stolen head. McSween was delighted with the acquisition of this damaging account book, thinking it would make a telling legal weapon to wield against Murphy & Co.

Billy had his doubts but he didn't voice them. McSween was the boss now, and if he said they should abide by the law, then the young cowboy was willing to give it a try. More than that; he would give it a helping hand.

Early next morning he and Fred Waite went over to Justice Wilson's office and Billy made a sworn statement against the men who had murdered Tunstall. Wilson was a pro-McSween man and he wrote out the warrants and gave them to Constable Antonio Martinez to serve. Billy and Waite volunteered to act as the constable's deputies. Arming themselves with rifles they strode down to Dolan's store and walked in the front door.

Most of Morton's bunch were there and they had no intention of surrendering to the constable. They claimed that they were also deputies of the law and that Martinez had no authority to arrest them. Wise old Sheriff Brady quickly resolved the moot matter by arresting the constable and his two deputies!

Surrounded by a ring of pistol barrels, Billy and his two friends were relieved of their weapons and locked up in Dolan's storeroom.

Martinez protested that he had warrants from the justice of the peace against every Dolan man in the store, and that Brady should be helping him to arrest those men—instead of arresting the town constable in the performance of his duty! Brady, cagey as ever, finally agreed to let Martinez go, but he refused to let him serve his warrants.

Tunstall was buried two days later behind his store. The legend workers take great delight in telling how a grim-faced Billy the Kid stood beside the open grave vowing vengeance against his friend's murderers while Dr. Ealy read the service. It sounds dramatic but it is not true. Billy and Waite were still under guard in Dolan's storeroom. Brady, in his spiteful way, refused to let them attend the funeral.

It was a slap in the face that Billy wouldn't forget.

Brady released his prisoners two days after the funeral, and Billy and Waite rejoined their friends in McSween's home. Dick Brewer had decided to turn the feud into open warfare. At McSween's advice he had had himself appointed special constable and had collected the warrants for Dolan's men from Martinez. His next act was to have Justice Wilson deputize the following men: Frank McNab, Doc Scurlock, Frank and George Coe, Charlie Bowdre, Billy Bonney, Hendry Brown, Fred Waite, Jim French, John Middleton, William McCloskey, Jake Scoggins, and "Dirty Steve" Stevens. This special posse was known as the Regulators, and they rode out of Lincoln on the first of March with the intention of bringing Tunstall's murderers to justice.

It is ironic to note that from the very onset of the Lincoln County War both factions were working as duly appointed lawmen. There was, however, this difference: the only official papers Brady's posse carried were the illegal writs of attachment on Tunstall's property; whereas Brewer's Regulators carried legal warrants issued by a justice of the peace. And yet in the end it was the Regulators who were considered to be the outlaws.

On March 6 the Regulators were joggling south along the Pecos. They forded the Rio Feliz in the early morning and approached the Rio Penasco ford at noon. Five of Dolan's gunhands were having a siesta smoke under the nearby cottonwoods.

Spotting Brewer's posse the five men sprang into their saddles and lammed for the west in a glory of dust, with the Regulators hot on their hoofs. The pony Tunstall had given Billy was a spunky mount and he soon racked into the lead of the chase. After about three miles of lathery riding two of the fugitives swung off to the right and went pell-mell for the hills.

Billy was close enough to recognize them and his heart gave a thump. The two riders were Bill Morton and Frank Baker! Yelling back at the posse to let the other three go, he spurred after his two sworn enemies.

Brewer, Waite, McNab, and Billy started to open fire as they rode, and Morton and Baker made the mistake of suddenly wheeling their nags about to fire back from their saddles. A broadside of Winchesters and Colts roared at them and both their horses went down in a tangled, thrashing clump.

The two fugitives sprang clear, Baker snatching out his carbine, and they ran dodging through the cattails and piled into a shallow dry sinkhole. The Regulators slung a circle around them and found cover, and a rifle-cracking siege began. But it was hopeless for Morton and Baker and they knew it. No food, no water, low on ammo—they waved a bandana just before sundown, calling for a parley.

Dick Brewer gave his promise to protect them if they would surrender, and both of them knew that he was a man of his word. They weren't so certain about the rest of the Regulators though. As they dropped their guns Frank Baker offered his hand to Billy.

"Hi, Billy."

"I don't know you," Billy said coldly, "and don't want to."

Most of the Regulators felt the same way about the two prisoners. Why haul these murderers back to Lincoln and hand them over to Brady who would promptly find some "legal" way to turn them loose? But Brewer had promised them his protection and Billy merely shrugged. He didn't like it but he would swallow it.

The posse and its prisoners spent the night in one of Chisum's line camps, and Morton, fearing that he and Baker would never reach Lincoln alive, wrote a farewell letter to his cousin in Virginia. The next day the posse made a stop at the Roswell store on the Hondo and Morton gave Ash Upson, who was the postmaster at that time, his letter to mail for him "just in case."

Morton's premonition was right. He and Baker were shot to death that same day at Agua Negra (Black Water) Spring. Exactly who did the shooting has never been established, though of course the myth spinners have gleefully given Billy the Kid full credit; but according to various witnesses, this could not be true.

Roughly, here is what happened. Billy, Brewer, and Bowdre were in the lead as the posse approached Agua Negra. Middleton and McCloskey were riding on either side of the prisoners, and the rest of the posse was strung out behind. William McCloskey, fearing that some of the Regulators intended to murder the prisoners, either slipped one of them his pistol and was promptly shot by Frank McNab who saw him do it—or one of the prisoners suddenly snatched McCloskey's pistol and shot him with it.

However it happened, there *was* a sudden shot and McCloskey toppled out of his saddle dead. Morton and Baker then made an abrupt break for freedom but were instantly riddled by the thirteen guns of the posse. Billy had no regrets about it. At least two of Tunstall's murderers had been crossed off the list.

Unknown to the Regulators at that time the man

who had fired the first bullet into Tunstall was already dead. On March 1 Tom Hill had tried to hold up a Cherokee Indian near Mesilla. The Indian had expressed his protest by drilling Hill with his rifle.

On the night of March 9 Dick Brewer slipped into Lincoln to pick up the latest news from McSween. It was all bad. Sam Axtell, the governor of New Mexico Territory (evidently a pro Santa Fe Ring man), had recently arrived at Fort Stanton, an army post ten miles west of Lincoln. The governor had refused to listen to McSween's plea for justice; instead he had aligned himself openly with Dolan and Brady, and had issued a proclamation which bluntly dismissed Justice of the Peace Wilson from his office.

This unwarranted act nullified Brewer's commission as a constable and turned his special posse into a vigilante group, which of course was not recognized by the law.

"Dick," McSween said, "you and your boys better take to the hills."

Brewer advised McSween to do the same. The lawyer saw the wisdom in this and made out his will that same night. Then he and Deputy Barrier (the Las Vegas deputy refused to let Brady get his hands on McSween) took off for the Pecos.

Brewer rode back to the Ruidoso and told his boys that they were in a bad way. Not only had Governor Axtell done his utmost to outlaw them, he had also given orders that the Negro troopers of the 9th Cavalry stationed at Fort Stanton give assistance to Sheriff Brady in tracking down the Regulators.

Billy had to laugh. So this was justice! Now they not only had the Santa Fe Ring, Dolan's hired gunmen and Brady's posse against them but the governor and the US Army as well! But no matter how hopeless the situation seemed, none of the Regulators were willing to crawfish. They still believed they were doing what was morally right. Tunstall's murderers had to receive their reckoning, and the Regulators intended to continue to serve their warrants, valid or not.

In order to elude and baffle Brady, now backed up by a detachment of cavalry, Brewer split his force into two groups. Billy headed for the hilly country west of the Hondo, taking with him Fred Waite, Hendry Brown, John Middleton, Jim French, and Charlie Bowdre.

The next three weeks were spent in playing a dangerous game of cross-tag. Brewer's group would suddenly appear on the Ruidoso and Brady's posse would give chase; then Billy's *compadres* would cross the sheriff's trail and lead the posse toward Rio Tularosa for a few days; and then Brewer would double back and divert the bewildered Brady once again.

It was interesting, even fun—but it was all building toward a violent climax. The day for McSween's embezzlement trial was drawing closer and closer, and Billy was certain that the righteous and foolhardy lawyer would appear in Lincoln to defend himself even though he suspected he was walking into a Dolan-laid trap.

As far as Billy was concerned the trial in Lincoln was just that: a trap to waylay and assassinate McSween. In fact, he and his five pals had heard from various sources that Brady was definitely set to ambush McSween on the morning of April 1, when the lawyer was due to arrive in town.

Acting on this information the six Regulators rode quietly up the Bonito riverbed on the night of March 31, slipped their horses into the adobe stable behind McSween's house, and entered the rear of the abandoned house to grab a few hours shuteye.

Come sunup they left the house and eased across the corral behind Tunstall's store. A plank fence squared off the rear of the building and the six men crouched down in the fence corner just east of the store. Tunstall's grave was only a couple of yards beyond the angle they were hiding in. They waited.

At nine a.m. Brady and his deputy George Hindman came strolling along the street with three other deputies tagging a short distance behind. The other three were Billy Mathews, John Long, and George "Dad" Peppin. They all carried Winchesters and Colts.

As the sheriff's party reached the east end of Tunstall's store the six Regulators rose and leveled their rifles over the top of the plank gate and cut loose with a crash of fire.

William Brady never knew what hit him. He went down in a heap. George Hindman was dead and didn't know it. He automatically ran a couple of yards before he crumpled. Mathews, Long, and Dad Peppin ran across the road and dodged behind the Cisneros house.

"Who's for getting some new rifles?" Billy asked. His old $10 Winchester wasn't worth owning. He had just fired a clean miss at Mathews.

None of his pals had the nerve to make a dash into the open road except the breed Fred Waite. He and Billy darted through the gate and ran into the street to retrieve the Winchesters that Brady and Hindman had dropped.

Mathews, Long, and Peppin immediately opened fire from behind the Cisneros house. Billy's hip was creased by a slug and Waite got a nick in his thigh. The two youths ran for cover, each carrying a new rifle. Supposedly, Billy's only comment on the affair was:

"Dammit, I'm sorry we didn't get Mathews."

The little band raced across the corral to McSween's stable, forked their ponies and went piling down the Bonito toward Rio Hondo. Though two of their party were suffering slight flesh wounds, they felt quite pleased with the day's work. The hated Brady, who had been like a festering thorn in their side, had been removed and George Hindman's name had been crossed off the list of Tunstall's wanted murderers.

They cut over to the Ruidoso to hole up for a while in San Patricio, where they were well received by the Mexican populace. These *pobres* had good reason to believe that the Regulators were fighting to protect them from the avaricious clutches of the despised Murphy & Co., and many of them had already avowed themselves as McSween supporters.

On April 2 a tall, rangy Irish boy from Texas rode into the plaza and introduced himself to Billy and the others. His name was Tom O'Folliard, he was eighteen, and he had left home to follow the adventure trail. Drifting into New Mexico he had picked up garbled accounts of the bloody feud raging in Lincoln County and had decided to come see what it was all about.

Billy and Tom were greatly alike inasmuch as they both had an effusive sense of humor which enabled them to accept danger as a sort of tongue-in-cheek joke. The big difference between them was that Billy was a natural leader, and Tom was a follower. The young Texan would stick to Billy to the tragic end—and even beyond. They were slated to lie side by side in a lonely plot of earth forever.

Chapter 5

On April 3 the Regulators came together in full force in the Sacramento Mountains to hold a council of war.

Dick Brewer, a young man of faultless principles, was deeply disturbed by the shooting of Brady and Hindman. To his mind Billy and his five compadres had acted rashly. They were already in enough trouble with the governor and the army, and now a reward of $200 for the "dead or alive" capture of any of the six men involved in the killing had been posted.

Brewer looked at it from a new angle, however, when he learned that Andy "Buckshot" Roberts was roaming around the Tularosa region in the role of a bounty hunter, hoping to collect the reward on one or more of the Regulators. Roberts had been one of Tunstall's murderers, and Brewer still had a warrant for his arrest. He decided there was no time like the present to settle the matter.

On April 4 the Regulators headed for Rio Tularosa to look for the man who was looking for them.

Late in the morning they arrived at Doc Blazer's

isolated mill, which was simply a long adobe house and a sawmill situated on the riverbank. The riders trooped into the house to see about some chow, and long about noon John Middleton came inside and said:

"A mighty well-armed *hombre* just came across the river on a mule. He's hitching down at the corral."

Nobody thought much of it and Frank Coe stepped outside to see who it was. He and Roberts met in the yard, and Coe grinned.

"Well, Andy, you sure walked yourself into a nice situation."

Roberts was a tough old desperado with a long criminal record including desertion from the US Army. Supposedly he had once fought a pitched battle with some Texas Rangers and had received the blast of a shotgun in his carcass; hence his nickname "Buckshot." He realized he had unwittingly walked himself into a pickle, but he had a rifle in his hands and was ready to shoot his way out.

"We've got a warrant for you," Frank said. "There's thirteen of us and you'd be a fool not to surrender peaceable."

Roberts replied he didn't care what they had—he wasn't about to surrender to Brewer's bunch. He knew what had happened to Morton and Baker when they were taken prisoner. He'd fight first. He hefted his Winchester to hip level. His left arm was so damaged by buckshot he couldn't raise a rifle to his shoulder.

Just then Brewer, Billy, Middleton, George Coe, Charlie Bowdre, and Tom O'Folliard came around the corner of the building. Bowdre instantly snatched for his Colt, calling:

"Throw up your hands, Roberts, or you're a dead man!"

"Not me, Mary Anne!" Roberts cried, and blazed

from the hip.

Bowdre fired at the same split second. Roberts' bullet ricocheted off Bowdre's belt buckle and clipped George Coe's right hand, mangling his trigger finger. Bowdre's slug caught Roberts smack in the stomach but didn't knock him down. Stumbling backwards the tough old badman blazed away wildly, blasting out rifle shots right and left. One of his slugs caught Middleton in the left lung and threw him to the ground. The rest of the Regulators scattered for the nearest cover in a frenzy of haste.

Gutshot or not, that old desperado was wicked!

Mortally wounded but still game, Roberts staggered into the house and dragged a thick mattress up to the front window. His Winchester was empty but he spotted an old buffalo gun—a .50 caliber Sharps rifle—by the door. He took this over to the window and sprawled on the mattress. Gasping with the searing pain in his guts, the old lobo was prepared to fight to the finish.

Doc Scurlock, Fred Waite, Hendry Brown, and three others had ducked behind the house, and Billy, Tom, Brewer, Bowdre, and the two Coes gathered below the riverbank. Brewer didn't realize how badly Roberts had been hit and he wanted to rush the house and get the mess over with. Charlie Bowdre thought they should wait until Roberts died from the fatal gutshot.

"I dusted him on both sides," he said. "He can't last long."

Brewer, who was usually the most rational man in the group, wouldn't listen. He told the others to stay there, and he crawled along the bank to the corner of the mill and got himself into position behind a pile of saw logs. The front of the house was 125 yards away. He took a sight with his rifle and whapped two shots through the distant front window. There was no answering fire.

Was Roberts already dead? Brewer, in uncharacteristic impatience, raised his head slightly to take another look at the house.

Buckshot Roberts wasn't quite dead. Lying in groaning agony on the doubled-up mattress, the barrel of the heavy Sharps resting on the window sill, he saw Brewer poke his head above the logs. His finger felt for the trigger as he drew a bead. Enough strength left for one last shot, Mary Anne . . .

The buffalo gun roared and Brewer pitched over backwards, the top of his head blown off. Never knew what hit him!

That was enough for the Regulators. Their leader was dead, Middleton was unconscious with a slug in his chest, and George Coe was on pins and needles with his shattered hand. Old Buckshot had won the day. Keeping carefully out of range of Roberts' window, Billy and the others put the two wounded men in a buckboard and set off for Frank Coe's Ruidoso ranch.

Doc Blazer buried Dick Brewer and Buckshot Roberts side by side the next day. The Lincoln County War was now six weeks old and nine combatants were already in their graves. It was only the beginning.

McSween's trial began on April 8, but none of the Regulators were able to attend. Frank McNab was their new leader and on his advice they stayed clear of Lincoln for fear of being shot down on the town street by some of Dolan's "deputies."

Judge Bristol, a Santa Fe Ring adherent, presided at the trial and it was quite apparent that he was deeply prejudiced against McSween. He openly vilified the lawyer in court and came as close as he could to calling him a thief and an embezzler without stating it in exact words. The grand jury, however, decided otherwise and McSween was exonerated and set free. But his acquittal came hand in hand with foreboding news . . .

During the trial Constable Martinez happened to overhear a brief conversation between Prosecuting Attorney Rynerson and Jimmy Dolan. Rynerson evidently realized that McSween was going to get off scot-free, and turning to Dolan, he said:

"Don't give up, Jimmy. Stick to that McSween crowd. I'll aid you all I can and will send you twenty men. Stick to the fight and give it to those rascals. That is the only way to win."

According to Martinez, when he passed this information on to the Regulators, Rynerson's reference about sending Dolan twenty men meant John Kinney's notorious outlaw band. Nearly all of Kinney's gang were under murder indictments, and they either did what Rynerson told them to or he would try them and send them to the gallows.

There was one ray of light for McSween's men. The county commissioners appointed John Copeland as the new Lincoln sheriff. Copeland was an innocuous man with little or no get-up-and-go to his nature, and he was inclined to be in favor of the McSweenites.

McSween's trial ended on April 24 and Frank McNab, lulled into a false sense of security by his boss' court victory and the appointment of Copeland as sheriff, made the mistake of relaxing his vigilance. He split the Regulators into four groups so that men like Scurlock, Bowdre, and the Coes could return to their ranches to take care of their chores.

A week later McNab rode down Bonito Canyon to meet Frank Coe and his in-law, Ab Sanders, at Fritz' Spring ranch about eight miles east of Lincoln. Without warning, twenty of Dolan's Seven Rivers riders (possibly led by Deputy Sheriff Peppin) opened fire on them from ambush.

The three startled men vaulted into their saddles

and tried to make a run for it up the draw, but the second blast of gunfire brought down McNab and Sanders, horses and all. Both men—Sanders plugged in the hip and ankle, McNab mortally wounded—crawled into the oak brush to find cover.

The third volley cut down Frank Coe's pony, and just as he was dragging himself clear Bob Olinger galloped up blazing away with his Colt. With bullets knocking up dirt all around him, Coe dodged into the rocks to make a stand with his six-shooter.

Coe knew he would have to throw in his hand when he ran out of ammo, so he agreed to surrender to Wallace Olinger, Bob's brother, under a promise of protection. Wallace he could trust—but Bob Olinger was a make-believe badman who wore his blond hair down to his shoulders like Wild Bill Hickok and Buffalo Bill Cody. Bob was out to make a name for himself as a gunfighter—even if he had to shoot defenseless men to do it.

Wallace took Coe's empty pistol and told him that Frank McNab was dead and Sanders was in a bad way. Coe appealed to his captors.

"He's a good man and it's a shame to let him die out here alone."

The Seven Rivers men were agreeable. They carried the wounded Sanders back to the ranch and sent for a doctor. The next day, May 1, they started for Lincoln with their prisoner.

The shooting of Frank McNab was out-and-out murder. There were no warrants for his arrest, and he had been shot from ambush while going about his own peaceable business. The Regulators had lost another leader, and to his dying day Billy the Kid believed that Bob Olinger had been mainly responsible for McNab's death. He made it a point to remember that he had a reckoning coming with Olinger.

Billy along with Tom, Fred Waite, Jim French,

Hendry Brown, George Coe, and a couple of others were camped just outside of Lincoln when Dolan's men came joggling up the road with their prisoner. George Coe saw them coming and he wasted no time in trying to effect the release of his cousin Frank.

Swinging up his rifle George clipped the lead rider, Bill Campbell, snap off his pony by putting a bullet through his right leg. The moment Campbell hit the dust the rest of the Seven Rivers men jumped for cover behind the outlying houses.

The Regulators were strung along the Bonito bank and they opened with a fusillade of rifles. Frank Coe and his guard Wallace Olinger were crouching near the Ellis house, and Regulator bullets were humming and snicking all around them. Frank didn't much like the idea of being accidentally shot by his own friends.

"Say, Wally," he suggested, "I wouldn't seriously object to being somewhere else right now."

Wallace wasn't feeling any too comfortable himself. He and his prisoner pulled back, skirted through the foothills, and came into town from the other end. Half a dozen Dolan men were in the Murphy store when Wallace entered with his prisoner and they were inclined to settle Frank's hash out of hand with a well-placed bullet.

Wallace said no. Doc Blazer had told him that Frank had tried to give Buckshot Roberts a chance to surrender on the day of the fight at the mill, and he figured one good turn deserved another. He took Frank upstairs and stayed with him in a corner room.

The sound of firing was growing heavier down at the east end of town and finally Wallace couldn't stand it any longer. He was tired of sitting there playing guard; he wanted to get into the fight. He stood up and tossed Frank a Colt pistol.

"Take care of yourself, Frank," he said and

walked out of the room. Talk about Western fair play!

"Where's Coe?" the Dolan men asked as he came downstairs.

"Upstairs," Wallace said.

A couple of them started to go up to get him, but Frank stood at the head of the stairs with the Colt in his hand and warned them to stay below. They gave in then, and all of them left to go join the fight. A few minutes later Frank walked out of the store, crossed over to the riverbed and made his way along it to his friends.

The gunfight fizzled out around noon and the Regulators mounted up and pulled back into the hills. It was the first time the two factions had clashed in force, and other than Bill Campbell's shattered leg it had been a bloodless encounter. But this was only the prelude to the big all-out battle that had been a long time in the making.

McSween was outraged when he learned of McNab's death. On May 3 he went to the new justice of the peace and secured warrants for the arrest of Bob Olinger, Bob Beckwith, and nineteen others who had taken part in the Fritz Spring ambush. The warrants were duly turned over to Sheriff Copeland to be served.

Jimmy Dolan had anticipated this move, and in order to checkmate it he had hurriedly brought John Kinney's twenty gunmen into town to back up his twenty-one riders who were now under indictment for murder. Realizing he didn't stand a chance of serving his warrants against an armed mob like that, Copeland rode to Fort Stanton to request military assistance.

A new post commander had just been appointed to the fort: possibly due to the machinations of Governor Axtell. He was a stubborn, opinionated, hard-drinking, fifty-three year old colonel named Nathan Dudley. He had recently been court-martialed and dismissed from the army for improper conduct at Fort Union, but some of his high-ranking friends had managed to have his sentence suspended.

Colonel Dudley will always remain an unaccountable figure in the Lincoln County War. Biased, prejudiced, callous to the point of being psychotic, he immediately showed a mulish determination to assist Murphy & Co. in squashing McSween's faction. It has never been proved that he was accepting bribes from Jimmy Dolan, yet it is revealing to note that the lawyer who defended him at his Fort Union court-martial was none other than U.S. District Attorney Tom Catron, the big wheel of the Santa Fe Ring.

Colonel Dudley agreed to give Sheriff Copeland military assistance, but at the same time he dispatched a letter to Murphy & Co. informing them of how he intended to handle the situation—meaning to Dolan's advantage.

A detachment of cavalrymen clattered into town on May 4, and Olinger, Beckwith, and the other nineteen indicted men cheerfully filed out of Murphy's store and surrendered to the law. The troopers herded them off to the fort to be placed under guard.

On May 6 McSween and two influential citizens of Lincoln, Juan Patron and Isaac Ellis, appeared at the office of the justice of peace to testify against Dolan's "deputies." To their vast consternation a lieutenant with a squad of troopers placed *them* under arrest!

Dolan had moved quickly. He had ordered Deputy Dad Peppin to drum up a false charge of conspiracy against the three witnesses, and Colonel Dudley had blithely ordered their arrest. A shrewd move. McSween and his two friends were held under guard at the fort for three days—long enough for the justice of the peace to declare the indictments against Dolan's men invalid because no testimony had been sworn against them. The killers were set free.

At the same time two of Juan Patron's Mexican friends were shot and killed from ambush along the road to Lincoln. No move was made to apprehend their killers. By now poor Copeland was so hamstrung by the army, the local judiciary, and Dolan's hired lawmen that he was at the point of becoming totally ineffectual.

Frustrated by the pseudolegal maneuverings of Dudley, Dolan, and Peppin, the Regulators were slowly and helplessly being driven into a deadly *cul-de-sac*. It was beginning to look as though they were doomed to be picked off by their enemies one by one, while the law and the army simply sat back and watched with a satisfied smirk.

There were now five warrants out for the arrest of William Antrim, alias William H. Bonney, for the deaths of William Morton, Frank Baker, William Brady, George Hindman, and Andrew Roberts. This was regardless of the fact that Billy had been deputized to capture Morton and Baker, that he had held a warrant for the arrest of Roberts *when Bowdre shot him*, and that he had been carrying warrants for two of Brady's men when Brady and Hindman were gunned down. According to his story, which he later testified to in court, he had not fired at either Brady or Hindman; instead, he had tried to hit Billy Mathews.

But all of this was immaterial to the one-sided law in Lincoln County. Next to eliminating McSween, the Dolan crowd urgently wanted to get Billy the Kid.

With Brewer and McNab gone the eighteen-year-old cowboy had suddenly become the new leader of the Regulators. He had not asked for the position, nor had any of the others thought to discuss it. They simply assumed that he should take command. They admired his dash and courage, liked the way he smiled at danger and shrugged off defeat, respected his inherent intelligence.

In the beginning when he would quietly suggest, "Suppose we ride to such-and-such place," his *compadres* Tom O'Folliard, Fred Waite, and Charlie Bowdre would instantly back him up, and before long the others came to accept Billy's suggestions as decisions. There is no record of what McSween thought about Billy's ascension to command.

Learning of the injustice McSween had suffered at Fort Stanton, Billy decided to balance the account by hitting Murphy & Co. where it would hurt the most. On May 14 the Regulators crossed the Pecos and struck Dolan's cow camp.

A short furious gunfight broke out and Dolan's riders were sent scampering on foot among the chaparral thickets. The Regulators triumphantly rounded up twenty-seven of Dolan's prize ponies and herded them toward the Ruidoso region to scatter them among the farms of their Mexican allies.

In retaliation Dolan made an appeal to Tom Catron to bring pressure on the governor, hoping to further hamstring the Regulators with more legal chicanery. The ultimate result of this request struck the McSweenites like a blow from a broadsword.

On May 28 Governor Axtell issued a proclamation which was plainly aimed at the hard-pressed Regulators. It read in part:

First: John H. Copeland, Esq . . . is hereby removed from the office of sheriff, and I have appointed George W. Peppin, Esq. sheriff of Lincoln County . . .
Second: I commend all men and bodies of men now under arms to disarm and return to their

homes and their usual pursuits, and so long as the present sheriff has authority to call upon U.S. troops for assistance, not to act as a sheriff's posse.

So now Dad Peppin, a Dolan-owned man from his Stetson down to his spurs, was the Law in the county, fully empowered to use the U.S. troops in any manner he saw fit. And of course the part in the proclamation that said"all bodies of men should disarm" merely meant that *the Regulators* should lay down their arms and disband. It was not intended to disarm John Kinney's outlaws or Dolan's gunmen.

It was a double-edged death sentence for the Regulators. If they dropped their weapons Dolan's men would shoot them down unarmed; if they continued to fight they would be declared outlaws and would be indicted for armed violence and murder and, when apprehended, be sentenced to the gallows.

Billy, hiding out at this time near San Patricio, had no idea what McSween would want to do about the proclamation but he knew what *he* was going to do. Governor or no governor, he wasn't ready to lay down his arms and let Dolan ride him under. His enemies could kill him, but they couldn't defeat him.

The rest of the Regulators were in accord with his decision. They had gone this far in the Lincoln County War, and now they were determined to see it through to the bloody end—win, lose, or draw.

Chapter 6

McSween did not know just how he should react to the proclamation. He was a harassed, confused man with a heavy sense of impending disaster hanging over him. Except for his now outlawed Regulators, it seemed that every man's hand was poised to strike him. The retaliatory violence his riders had caused had gained him very little, and his desperate motions toward legal justice had netted him nothing.

He felt that he was a marked man. One way or another Dolan would find the means to destroy him. It was only a matter of time.

There was one spark of hope. Certain impartial witnesses of the feud had seen to it that news of the unjust situation reached Washington D. C. These unbiased reports led President Rutherford B. Hayes to suspect that Murphy & Co. were making illegal use of the Territorial law and the US Army. To firmly establish the true facts, he sent a special investigator from the Department of Justice to New Mexico. This agent's name was Frank W. Angel, and he was destined to deliver the deathblow to the powerful Santa Fe Ring.

But this investigation would take time. And McSween and the Regulators were running very short on that precious commodity.

In mid-June McSween dispatched a Mexican rider to find Billy and to tell him to come to Lincoln as soon as possible. With characteristic bravado Billy, Bowdre, O'Folliard, Scurlock, Hendry Brown, and Middleton (now recovered from his wound) cantered into town a couple of days later. They caught Sheriff Peppin with his pants down.

Assuming that Billy the Kid would never have the nerve to appear openly in town, Peppin had his posses scattered over half of the county fruitlessly beating the mesquite thickets for the hideout of the Regulators.

It is said that Billy and his pals rode up to Murphy's store and greeted Peppin who was standing alone on the porch.

"Hello, Dad," Billy supposedly said. "I hear you have some warrants for me and my *amigos*. Hand 'em over and we'll save you the time of looking for us."

"Some other time will do, Billy," Peppin said, and hastily made tracks into the store.

McSween told Billy that he had decided to place himself under the protection of the Regulators rather than to take his chances by remaining in the hostile town. This was only common sense to Billy and he and the others conducted their noncombatant boss out of Lincoln in an armed escort.

Dad Peppin, fuming inwardly, watched them go from one of The House's windows. Then he quickly dispatched riders to all points of the compass to call back his various posses. He also sent a request to Colonel Dudley for the use of a detachment of troopers. The colonel promptly sent him a captain and thirty-five men.

To Peppin's mind this was the ideal opportunity to annihilate all the ringleaders of the hated McSween faction.

Peppin's groups suddenly clashed headlong with McSween, Billy, Scurlock, and seven other Regulators. Billy's side beat them to the draw and scattered the possemen with a broadside of Colts. Deputy John Long had his horse shot from under him and had to chase after his panicky men on foot.

Learning of the incident, Peppin quickly consolidated his forces and moved toward San Patricio, which he knew was a favorite Regulator hangout. The ambitious sheriff was already licking his chops over the sweet taste of success. Eliminating McSween would make him the fair-haired boy of the Santa Fe Ring, and killing Billy the Kid would make him the most famous man in the Territory.

McSween's fighters had just started to decamp from San Patricio on the morning of June 28, when Peppin's posse and the US troopers came thundering into the peaceful little Mexican village. Outnumbered three or four to one, the Regulators immediately deployed themselves among the cottonwoods to make a last stand.

Just as Peppin was preparing to make an overwhelming assault a rider from Fort Stanton galloped up and delivered a dispatch to Captain Carroll in command of the detachment of troopers.

Acting upon the first information received from Special Investigator Angel, the United States Congress had passed a bill which prohibited the use of U.S. soldiers in the quelling of any civil strife. The order came direct from the War Department.

Upon receipt of this startling message Captain Carroll promptly started his detachment of cavalry back to the fort, leaving the stunned Peppin and his posse holding the bag.

Quickly remounting, the Regulators gleefully rode

off toward the Pecos. All of them thought it was a great joke on old Dad Peppin.

It is known that on or about July 2 Billy and a few Regulators had a run-in with some of Dolan's riders from Seven Rivers. The prevailing story centers around Charlie Bowdre.

Charlie had been riding point since early morning and had gone on ahead into a fertile canyon. Suddenly Billy and the others heard a short outburst of shots and they spurred through the canyon mouth, coming to a halt in a narrow grassy valley with high timbercapped rock walls. Bowdre had run into Dolan's men and exchanged a few shots with them before being captured.

Billy knew what his friend's chances were of reaching Lincoln alive as a prisoner, and he instantly decided to free Charlie at any cost. With a loud Indian yell he dug in his rowels and Old Grey bolted forward like an arrow, Tom, Waite, and the others coming right behind him.

The Seven Rivers men rushed to a clump of green, a waterhole, and made a stand in the willows. Billy held straight on. He heard a shot, then a spate of shots, and close about him the dust flew up in little fountains. The willows were spitting fire now and the Regulators fanned out and found cover.

The bloodless battle was a standoff, but Dolan's men were boxed in and would have to ask for terms. Here again legend tries to make use of Jesse Evans by having him hold a parley with Billy. This could not possibly be, because Jesse was standing trial for Tunstall's murder in Mesilla on July 2, and did not return to Lincoln until the middle of the month.

Whoever the leader was—possibly Bob Beckwith, a young Pecos rancher only a year older than Billy— he said he would surrender Bowdre if the Regulators would let him and the other Seven Rivers men go. It was agreed and the two groups parted, the Regulators riding off jauntily with Charlie Bowdre, leaving the greatly relieved Seven Rivers men behind.

Two days later the Regulators celebrated the Fourth of July, 1878, with another gunfight. They had reached John Chisum's South Spring ranch the night before and had been made welcome by Chisum's eighteen-year-old niece Sally. Uncle John himself was still keeping his skirts clean by staying clear of Lincoln County. Throughout the entire protracted ordeal he seemed quite satisfied to let McSween and the Regulators do his fighting for him.

A bunch of Dolan's riders attacked the ranch the first thing in the morning, and Billy and his pards climbed up to the flat roof of the adobe house and fought them off with Winchesters. Again there was a lot of noise but no bloodshed.

Sally Chisum was greatly taken with the young captain of the Regulators. When she first heard that the infamous Billy the Kid had arrived at the ranch she had gone into a mild panic, picturing him as some kind of bloodthirsty ogre. Instead she was introduced to a good-looking, clear-eyed boy who approached her with a polite smile. She was amazed when they shook hands to find that his hand was as small as her own.

During the week that the Regulators spent at Chisum's ranch, Sally and Billy became good friends, indulging in long rides along the river and occasional perch-fishing sprees. She soon came to understand why the local *pobres* always referred to the quiet, unassuming, friendly boy as *"muy simpatico"*. In bald translation it is merely "very sympathetic," but it means much more than that to Mexican-speaking people. It is the highest tribute they can pay to a man's compassion and empathy.

On July 11 the Regulators took to the high timber again, striking north along the Pecos and then west into the Capitans. The harassed McSween was physically and morally wrung out. Living in the saddle, fleeing along the back trails, dodging in and out of gunfights—this was not his kind of life. Nor could he see any advantage to such a haphazard existence. He made a fatal decision.

He would return home and settle the feud in Lincoln. Legal or illegal, right or wrong, win or lose, this bloody business had to culminate. It had been raging across the county for nearly five months now and twelve men, good and bad, had been blasted into Boot Hill by Colt law. It must not be allowed to continue. They would gather together all their allies move into town, and prepare for the grand showdown.

On the night of July 14 McSween and his men rode up the Bonito and turned into the feud-stricken town. The one long dark street was deceptively quiet, slumbering peacefully without knowledge of the horrific violence which was shortly to explode from one end of Lincoln to the other. The Regulators stabled their ponies and trooped into the lawyer's house to be greeted by Susan McSween.

"I'm not leaving any more," McSween told his frightened wife.

He signed his own death warrant with those words.

Shortly before dawn on Monday, July 15, Martin Chavis rode into Lincoln with twenty-five Mexican-Americans, all McSween partisans. McSween, Billy, Scurlock, and Chavis held a council of war and decided to split their forty men into five unequal groups; each group would establish itself in a key position in the town and wait to see what action Dolan and Peppin would take to dislodge them.

By sunup the McSweenites had virtually seized control of Lincoln, their trained rifles commanding two-thirds of the long street. Along the eastern approach eight riflemen were posted in the Ellis house; five more were in Juan Patron's large abode; and Martin Chavis had ten men with him in the Montano building which was directly behind the Stockton saloon. All the horses were herded into the Ellis corral.

Tunstall's store was in the center of the town and Charlie Bowdre, George Coe, and Hendry Brown were inside it with the doors and windows barricaded. Just west of their position was McSween's house. There were thirteen men in the lawyer's fortified home: Alexander McSween, Billy Bonney, Doc Scurlock, Tom O'Folliard, Jim French, Jim Davis, Harvey Morris (a twenty-year-old law student), Vincente Romero, Ignacio Gonzales, Francisco Zamora, Florencio Chavez and Jose Chavez y Chavez, and Hijinio Salazar who was barely fifteen years old.

There were also two women in the house—Susan McSween and her sister Mrs. Shield, plus four small children belonging to Mrs. Shield. Susan refused to leave her husband, and Mrs. Shield would not leave her sister.

Though Dolan and Peppin had been caught napping they did not remain idle for long. Their first move was to rush a handful of riflemen to the Torreon, a circular stone-and-adobe tower east of Tunstall's store. The Torreon was nearly twenty feet high and the flat roof was protected by a thick parapet. Saturnino Baca's house was right next door and Dolan's men intended to use it as a source of supply for their food and water.

Realizing the threat this posed, Billy prompted McSween to write an ultimatum to Baca warning him that he must either vacate his property at once or suffer the consequences.

Poor Baca had a bedridden wife who could not be moved, and he appealed to McSween for clemency.

McSween promised to leave the Bacas alone providing they would not supply Dolan's men with food and water. This mutual agreement completely isolated the riflemen in the tower.

Meanwhile Dolan and Peppin were frantically collecting their gunfighters, and by noon they had nearly forty men in town. They divided them into two groups, one party to hold the Wortley Hotel some hundreds of yards west of McSween's house, the other party stationed in Murphy's store across the street from the hotel.

Dad Peppin then sent his deputies, John Long and Marion Turner, along the arroyo to the rear of the McSween house. John Kinney, the outlaw chief, accompanied them. Reaching the corral behind the stable Deputy Long called that he had warrants for nearly every man in the house and store, and demanded that they come out with their hands in the air.

Billy was standing in the rear room of the west wing and he laughed and told Long to go jump in the Bonito with his warrants. Kinney was for opening fire and starting the fight then and there, but Turner, a sensible and moderate man, said no. They pulled back and returned to Murphy's store.

A nervous waiting period began. Who would fire the first shot?

Late that afternoon Jesse Evans and a handful of Seven Rivers riders came racking into town from the east end, successfully running the gauntlet past the fortified Ellis, Patron, and Montano buildings. With their Colts in hand they galloped by Tunstall's store —still no one fired at them. Then they were abreast of McSween's house, and for one static moment Billy the Kid and Jesse Evans glanced at each other.

Billy's Winchester swung up, Jesse's Colt threw down. Both guns blazed simultaneously—Jesse's slug knocking splinters out of the window frame by

Billy's head, Billy's bullet whipping Jesse's hat from his head. And then as the riders went pounding on down the street in a marvel of flung dust, nearly eighty rifles exploded furiously from one end of Lincoln to the other.

The Four Days' Battle was on.

Chapter 7

Sporadic gunfire continued all though that Monday night and picked up its pace on Tuesday morning, July 16. Then it settled into desultory firing as Dolan snipers wormed through the brush and rock-clad hills along the south side of town. They sniped at the Patron and Montano buildings, while their allies in Murphy's store and hotel banged away at McSween's house.

While bullets whacked on the adobe walls and the wooden shutters and windows threw off jagged splinters and shards of glass, Billy and the others maintained a steady answering fire. It is on record that Susan McSween and her sister busied themselves in the sheltered kitchen cooking meals for the grub-hungry fighting men.

Alexander McSween sat slumped in a mood of despair, apathetically reading his Bible; a righteous and ineffectual man looking for spiritual guidance in a lead holocaust. Once Billy offered him a rifle but the lawyer shook his head. To lift a hand in anger against a fellow human being was abhorrent to his mild nature. He returned to the Good Book.

He was the only man out of the possible eighty combatants in town who felt that way. The others were set on wiping each other out. But to Dolan's mind the "wiping out" of the enemy was taking far too long. He told Peppin to write to Colonel Dudley and request help. Dad Peppin worded his appeal shrewdly:

> Mostly all the men for whom I have US warrants are in town, and are being protected by A.A. McSween and a large party of his followers . . . They are resisting, and it is impossible for me to serve the warrants. If it is in your power to loan me one your howitzers, I am of the opinion the (Regulators) . . . would surrender without a shot being fired.

He wasn't asking for much—merely the use of a cannon to dislodge the Regulators from their strongholds! But Dudley was hampered by the binding War Department order which forbade him to interfere in a civil disturbance. He wrote Peppin an apologetic note and dispatched it with Trooper Berry Robinson.

Robinson stupidly rode smack down the beleaguered street, and a stray bullet fired by either a Dolan or a McSween man came within his proximity. Dad Peppin immediately made the most of this incident, informing the colonel that the McSweenites had deliberately tried to shoot a US soldier.

This was the opening Dudley needed to throw his military weight against the McSween faction. A poorer excuse for an unjust act would be hard to find, but Dudley was never restrained by scruples. He ordered Captain Blair to move into Lincoln the next day with a detachment of troopers, supposedly to investigate the "Private Robinson Incident."

Wednesday morning, July 17, was ushered in with a cloudless sky and a dazzling sun. The heat hammered mercilessly at the embattled town as two sweating Dolan men, Charlie Crawford and Lucio Montoyo, snaked along the slope of the rocky hill behind the Montano house They were looking for a square shot at one of Martin Chavis' men who were sprawled behind the roof parapet 900 yards away.

One of Chavis' men, Fernando Herrera, had been studying the hillside for nearly an hour, watching the slow, labored progress of the two Dolan sharpshooters. Herrera bore the reputation of being the best marksman in Lincoln; still—900 yards was over half a mile, and that would require some shooting. But—*quién sabe*, who knows? Maybe it could be done.

Raising his long-range buffalo rifle over the parapet, he took a careful squint along the barrel and set up the lead Dolan sniper in his sights. His far-off target was as small as an ant and it was moving in and out of the brush and boulders. Very slowly Herrera compressed his right hand, squeezing the trigger.

Plam! The shot sped away and almost in the same second Charlie Crawford dropped his rifle, screamed, and plunged over the brow of a cliff, rolling, rolling all the way down the hillside and into a stalky cornfield south of the Montano house. Herrera's amazing shot—unparalleled in frontier history—had torn through Crawford's hips from right to left.

Lucio Montoyo, stunned to the very taproots of his soul(how could *any*one hit a half-hidden, moving target at 900 yards?), went piling on down the face of the hill in a mad dash for Murphy's store. Crawford, mortally wounded, lay out in the boiling July sun for hours, groaning and calling feebly for help. None of Dolan's men had the courage to go aid him.

It was noon when Captain Blair and his troopers clattered into town. The rifle fire on both sides instantly ceased and all the combatants took time out to eat and relax while they waited to see what the army would do.

Actually this so-called Military Board of Inquiry had already reached a foregone conclusion: the McSween faction was guilty of having fired on Private Robinson. But to give the sham procceddings an air of legality, Blair came to McSween's house and called the lawyer to the door for an examination.

McSween of course denied Peppin's charge that the Regulators had fired at the soldier, but Blair was content to believe that they had, and nothing the lawyer or the others could say would make him change his mind. The mock inquiry was abruptly ended when one of Peppin's deputies informed the captain that Crawford was lying at the foot of the south hill in a bad way.

Blair and Army Surgeon Appel went into the standing cornfield and found the mortally wounded sniper. Loss of blood and exposure to the brutal sun had nearly finished him. The two officers carried him down to the street and sent for an army ambulance. Crawford was in a deep state of shock when he was carried off to the fort hospital. He never regained consciousness.

With the departure of the cavalry, McSween experienced a sense of relief. He had been afraid that Dudley intended to interfere on Peppin's behalf. Now it looked to him as if the colonel meant to abide by the order from the War Department. Perhaps his prayers were being answered after all.

Late that afternoon young Ben Ellis, a noncombatant, went to the corral behind his home to feed the Regulators' horses. A sniper's bullet clipped him in the neck and he staggered back to the house streaming blood. When darkness shifted over Lincoln, two of the riflemen posted in the Ellis house waded up the Bonito to the back of Tunstall's store. The minister, Dr. Ealy, and his family were living in two spare rooms of the closed store.

Dr. Ealy said he would return with the two men to see what he could do for young Ben, but the moon was up when they tried to slip across the corral to reach the arroyo and Dolan's riflemen in the Torreon opened fire on them. The three men were driven back into the store and held there for the night.

The whorling sun soared over the rifle-crackling town on Thursday morning, July 18. Dr. Ealy, accompanied by Mrs. Ealy and their two children, stepped out of the store and proceeded to walk down the deserted street. The firing stopped short. Everyone—the Regulators in the four barricaded houses, the riflemen in the Torreon, the sharpshooters crouching on the hillside—watched the valiant little troop stride boldly along on its errand of mercy.

The Ealy quartet reached the Ellis house without incident, and Dr. Ealy treated young Ben's wound. In a short while the doctor and his small family came outside and started back down the long dusty street. Still not a shot was fired and the Ealys were allowed to reenter their home in peace. *Then* a rifle cracked, and another, and the battle was on again.

But it had lost a great deal of its original impetus. There was a noticeable slack in the Dolan-Peppin gunfire. The riflemen in the ovenlike Torreon were suffering from a lack of food and water, the snipers on the torrid hillside lived in fear of Herrera's deadly buffalo rifle, and Kinney's rough-and-ready outlaws in the hotel were growing surly because the battle seemed to be fizzling into a boring stalemate.

The Regulators' rifles still commanded two-thirds of Lincoln, and to their thinking victory was just over the horizon. Before long the men in the Torreon would have to surrender, the snipers would abandon the hills, and Kinney's bunch would probably evacuate town in disgust. It was merely a matter of sweating it out.

Jimmy Dolan was doing just that, sweating in desperation. What was wrong with Dudley? Was he going to come help Peppin or not? Unable to contain himself any longer he mounted up and rode over to the fort to see the colonel.

Yes, Dudley certainly wanted to help him and Peppin, but he feared the Robinson incident might not prove to be sufficient enough grounds for him to order US troops into Lincoln. He was leery of the War Department's censure.

Cannily Dolan approached the problem from a new angle. Most of the civilians had fled town at the beginning of the battle, but there were still some women and children who had elected to remain in their homes. Surely *they* had the right to expect Dudley's protection? This could only refer to Susan McSween, Mrs. Shield, Mrs. Ealy, and the Shield and Ealy children, who were all obviously on McSween's side. But Dolan and Dudley didn't concern themselves with that minor detail; they were looking for an opportunity and any pliable excuse would serve.

Dudley called in his officers and had them sign a statement which in effect said they all believed that the army should occupy Lincoln in order to safeguard the lives and property of the civilians. Dudley was cautiously covering all his bets, just in case the War Department should later misconstrue his decision and conduct.

Dolan returned from Fort Stanton in high spirits, and that night Andy Boyle, formerly a British soldier and now a freelance gunman, crawled down the arroyo and into the Torreon to tell the riflemen the good news. All they had to do was hold out a little while longer, he told them. Tomorrow luck would start to swing in their direction.

It did just that. It swung with a vengeance.

Gunfire greeted the dawn of Friday July 19, as Dolan's men began to pepper McSween's house with renewed energy. Although the bulk of the Regulators were holding the Montano, Patron, and Ellis houses, Dolan and Peppin concentrated most of their efforts against the McSween house and store, knowing that the lawyer and the majority of his best fighters were holed up in those two positions.

If Dolan and Peppin played their cards right they would not only settle McSween once and for all, they would also wipe out most of the ringleaders of the Regulators. It is easy to picture Jimmy Dolan at this point beside himself with exultant anticipation. He could already envision his worst enemies, McSween, Billy the Kid, Charlie Bowdre, Doc Scurlock, George Coe, Tom O'Folliard, Jim French, and Hendry Brown, lying dead in the street.

The thirteen men inside McSween's house were also in an elated mood. They felt that this was going to be their lucky day. Surely most of Dolan's men would throw in their hands soon and pull out of the game. McSween himself was so confident of ultimate victory that he sat down to dash off a note to Ash Upson in Roswell:

> Dear Ash: Please send me $3.00 in stamps. I am here O.K. I suppose you hear queer versions. Right will triumph.

He was never more wrong in his short life. Right was not given the opportunity to triumph.

Some time after ten a.m. a Dolan lookout posted on top of Murphy's store yelled that a great cloud of dust was coming along the west road from the direction of the fort. Maybe a minute later a McSween lookout crouching on the flat roof of the lawyer's house called down the same news to his friends.

The men inside the house looked at each other with blank expressions. It could mean only one

79

thing.

They were right; shortly before eleven Colonel Dudley rode into town at the head of his cavalrymen. They paused for a moment before the Wortley Hotel, where Dudley and Peppin held a short confab, and then the mounted column rode clittery-clack on down the street.

From behind sheltered windows Billy and his *compadres* watched the blue-clad Negro troopers clop by the house. In their van was a mounted Gatling gun and two rolling twelve-pounder howitzers. Eight officers and thirty-five troopers in all. The little army moved down to the east end of town and turned into a vast vacant lot directly across the road from the Montano and Patron buildings. They began to set up camp.

Other than the jingle-jank of the troopers' equipment a catch-breath silence gripped the disputed town. As far as Billy was concerned the arrival of the army had torn it for his side. Dudley would now make it his business to see that the Regulators lost the battle.

He didn't let this change of luck dampen his spirits. He had joined the feud because he liked a good fight and now it looked as if he was really going to get one. He winked at Tom O'Folliard and slapped a couple of the dispirited Mexicans on the back. After that he and Tom prowled from window to window, whistling unconcernedly as they observed the activity out in the street.

It was very warlike activity. Colonel Dudley, with his usual lack of fair play, lost no time in posting one of his howitzers in the street before the Montano building. This, Billy thought, was a rather obvious gesture: get out or be blown out!

Shortly Martin Chavis, Juan Patron, and Isaac Ellis left their respective fortresses and entered the cavalry camp to talk with Dudley. The colonel did not care to discuss the matter with them. He tersely informed them that if any shots came from their three houses, thus endangering the lives of his soldiers, he would immediately open fire on them with his howitzers.

Having delivered his one-sided ultimatum, he then posted his soldiers along the street *between* the Montano building and the Torreon. If the Regulators in their barricaded houses fired just one shot at Dolan's men in the tower they would be blown apart by the cannons.

This high-handed action effectively nullified the usefulness of twenty-five McSweenites. There was nothing they could do but to vacate their positions and pull out of town. They disappeared down the Bonito in the early afternoon. A few of them, such as Fred Waite, Frank Coe, and John Middleton, doubled back through the hills north of the river to see if they could find some way to help the thirteen men trapped in McSween's house.

As soon as the main body of McSween allies quitted the town Bob Beckwith, the nineteen-year-old Seven Rivers man who had helped kill Tunstall, went into Murphy's store and got two cans of coal oil. What happened shortly after that almost appears to be a part of a concerted plan formed by Dolan, Peppin, and Dudley.

Legend loves to tell how Colonel Dudley himself now approached McSween's besieged house to deliver his ultimatum to the harassed lawyer in person, and that they held a lengthy debate in the dooryard. It is not true. Roughly, this is what happened:

Having disposed of Martin Chavis' men, Dudley seized the initiative by ordering the justice of the peace to issue a warrant against McSween for the attempted murder of Private Robinson! The warrant (illegal, because Robinson's case was a federal matter) was signed and handed to Deputy Marion

Turner to execute. Turner, with a bodyguard of troopers, proceeded to the front of McSween's house and called upon the lawyer to surrender himself to the law.

"Go on," Billy called back. "We got warrants for some of you!"

"All right!" Turner yelled. "But we have cannons and we'll blow your old house to pieces if you don't comply with the colonel's orders!"

Billy told him what he could do with his cannons, and Turner stalked away muttering to himself. The troopers remained in the street and more of them began to gather around the besieged house. McSween wrote a note of protest to Dudley:

> Would you have the kindness to let me know why soldiers surround my house? Before blowing up my property, I would like to know the reason.

In reply Dudley wrote a sardonic and callous note and dispatched it with one of his officers. McSween and his wife and Billy came to the door to read the colonel's answer and to talk to the courier.

"The colonel wishes you to be informed that he is here to protect the lives and property of the citizens," the officer said. "Furthermore, you must cease firing at once."

"We will willingly cease firing," McSween replied, "if Dolan's and Peppin's men will do the same. Otherwise we would be murdered."

"The army has not authority over Sheriff Peppin. Either lay down your weapons or suffer the consequences. If your men fire one shot over the heads of our soldiers, we will reply with our howitzers."

The officer about-faced himself and marched away. Billy had to laugh. It was the same old story: the Regulators should sheepishly lay down their arms to make it easy for Dolan's crowd to kill them. How one-way could an ultimatum be?

Jimmy Dolan was pretty certain that Billy and his gang would refuse to abide by Dudley's decree, and he had laid his plans accordingly. While McSween and the others were gathered in the front of the house talking to the army officer, Dolan sent John Long, Buck Powell, and Andy Boyle down the arroyo to the back of the McSween house. They were carrying a clutch of newspapers and wood shavings, and Bob Beckwith's two cans of coal oil.

Chapter 8

It was now three p.m.

Knowing that the rear of the McSween house was momentarily unguarded, Long, Powell, and Boyle raced across the backyard, shoved open the kitchen door, heaved in their load of combustible trash and doused it with the coal oil. One of them struck a match. A little blue peak of flame trembled, turned yellow, and began to lick at the papers and shavings.

As the arsonists started back across the yard, Bowdre, Brown, and George Coe spotted them from the rear of Tunstall's store. They immediately opened fire and the three Dolan men scattered like a covey of quail. Andy Boyle piled over the adobe wall that separated the backyard from the small patio between the two wings of the house and ducked out of sight.

Powell and Long were not so fortunate. They made a run for the gateway in the four-foot-high adobe wall in the north end of the yard but were cut off by the hail of bullets whacking around them. They veered to the right and charged into the small outhouse standing in the northeast corner of the yard.

Hearing the shooting, Billy and the others ran through the eastwing and discovered the fire in the kitchen. The flames had barely taken hold and they were able to beat it out. It was then Tom O'Folliard realized that two Dolan men were trapped in the outhouse. This seemed like the joke of the century to Tom and he proceeded to pump lead through the thin clapboard walls of the privy.

With Tom's bullets splintering through the boards there was nothing Long and Powell could do but tear up the two-seater plank and leap down into the sewer trap. It was a loathsome place to have to spend the day but Tom wouldn't let them out.

Meanwhile, Andy Boyle had crossed the patio and hopped into the stable yard behind the west wing. Unseen by the men who were busy putting out the fire in the other wing, he quickly piled a batch of old shingles and papers on the wooden steps by the back door and touched them off with a match.

A warm west wind was breathing at the house and it quickly fanned the little flames into a crackling fire which began to devour the door and floor planking. By the time the warning smoke came coiling into the other rooms it was too late to do anything about the fire. It was snapping across the entire floor, lapping up the adobe walls and licking at the heavy ceiling timbers. Room by room it slowly advanced through the west wing.

Billy and the others pulled back into the hot, hazy living room and looked at each other bleakly. They were caught like mice in a trap. An uncontainable fire raging inside the house, a ring of armed enemies waiting outside. McSween, nearly at his wits' end, resorted to his Bible. All else had failed him. Billy rolled a cigarette, contemplating their slim chances.

The house had ten main rooms and it was made of sturdy adobe in a long U shape. Unless the wind picked up it would take quite a while for the fire to destroy every room, and it would have to follow the plan of the house—down the west wing, across the three front rooms, then up the east wing—with the defenders retreating from room to room until they reached the rear kitchen. By then it would be dark. That would be the time to make a run for it.

His spirits soared. It was going to be a cracking good fight after all. And so what if they were gunned down? Nobody lives forever. He grinned, listening to Tom's rifle bang away at the outhouse. There was one *hombre* at least who was having the time of his brief life.

A blazing chunk of the roof crashed down and Billy stooped over and lighted his cigarette from it. "Much obliged," he said, and he winked at young Hijinio Salazar.

It was four p.m. and the Dolan-Peppin men were beginning to press in on the besieged house from all sides. On the west Kinney's boys slipped into the widely separated one-room adobe houses of Schon and Mills; on the north Dolan's snipers hunkered in the hills above the Bonito; his riflemen were still in the Torreon to the east, and now more sharpshooters took over the shanties of Cisneros and Stanley which were directly south of McSween's house. Pumping their Winchesters, they sent continuous streaks of lead at the burning house.

One of the most persistent and absurd legends of the Lincoln County War enters at this point. It concerns Mrs. McSween and her piano.

The myth makers delight in retelling how Susan McSween, with her home burning around her and her husband slated for sudden death, "threw herself on the stool at the keyboard" and began to pound out a soul-stirring war song, and how Billy and the others gathered around to sing patriotic songs while

Dolan bullets zinged through the smoky room, peppered the piano, and shattered the keyboard under Mrs. McSween's flying and talented fingers!

No doubt this sort of dramatic inventiveness is very inspiring, but there is not one word of truth in it. Mrs. McSween was far too frightened and distracted to play *The Star Spangled Banner* or anything else on the piano, and Billy and the other men were too busy firing from the windows to stop and hold a family circle songfest.

By five p.m. Mrs. McSween had reached the end of her tether. Something had to be done to save her husband and his men. She slipped through the front door and ran down the street to the cavalry camp. Contrary to the vivid fable which has her boldly sashaying down the street with bullets snipping through her skirts, no one fired a shot in her direction. Shooting at women was not in keeping with the Code of the West.

Colonel Dudley and John Kinney were sitting in the command tent with a jug of redeye. Mrs. McSween appealed to Dudley as an officer and gentleman to save her husband and his friends, but Dudley rudely informed her that he could not interfere with the local law; he was there in town merely to protect the civilians.

She asked him why didn't he do it then? Why did he and his soldiers simply stand around and watch her home burn up with thirteen men trapped inside it? Dudley bruskly replied that the men in her home were outlaws and that they should surrender themselves to Sheriff Peppin.

"Will you give them your protection if they do submit to arrest?"

No, he would not. The responsibility rested with the local authorities. It was the sheriff's duty to protect any civilian arrested in a civil disturbance, not Dudley's. Outraged by his blunt callousness, Mrs.

87

McSween lost control of herself.

"I can see through your whole intention!" she screamed at him. "I expect nothing else than that my husband will be killed in his own house. Even if they have a warrant for my husband, they will not arrest him. They want to kill him—and so do you!"

The irate colonel ordered a sentry to remove Mrs. McSween from his tent. He refused to speak another word to her. Defeated and distressed the poor woman returned to her burning home. Most of the west wing was now destroyed and Dolan's men were churning rifle bullets through the crumbling walls which shot up towers of flame as they fell in. The US troopers loafed in the street and watched. Fine show!

At six p.m. Fred Waite, Middleton, and a few others came down an arroyo on the far side of the Bonito and began taking potshots at the Dolan snipers who were spread out along the shadow-slanted riverbed. Peppin immediately sent out most of his possemen to chase them down, and the little band had to pull back into the hills to find cover.

That was the last hope the thirteen trapped men had for outside assistance. Now they were definitely on their own.

Dusk spread slowly over the little valley and fat rust-colored clouds of smoke rose into the lowering sky. The living room was going up like a fiery torch, and the desperate defenders had to retreat into the east wing, herding along Mrs. Shield's wide-eyed little children.

Not quite five rooms to go now.

The handful of Mexican-Americans were thinking it might be wise to surrender and take their chances with Peppin's men. Billy shook his head. No sense in being shot dead with your empty hands in the air; much better to go down fighting. *Viva valiente*!

88

Long live courage!

Tom O'Folliard and Doc Scurlock backed him up. They were eager to make a dash and a fight for it. Billy turned to Mrs. McSween who was sitting mutely with her totally dejected husband.

"I expect, ma'am," Billy said, "you better leave now. A dress ain't very good to make a run in."

She stared at the young Regulator for a long moment, and then nodded her head. She knew it was time to part from her husband. They embraced quietly, not knowing quite what to say to one another. They both felt it was a final goodby.

Dr. Ealy requested a few minutes truce and that great defender of civil liberty, Colonel Dudley, sent some troopers to the McSween house to give the women and children safe conduct.

Mrs. McSween and Mrs. Shield and her four children walked out of the burning house and crossed the lot to Tunstall's store, where they joined the Ealys. The soldiers conducted them down the long shadow-clustered street. Then the firing resumed.

Now it was dark out and the east wing was alight like a box of matches. Blazing timbers crashed down, smoking walls toppled inward sending up dazzling sprays of sparks, and the throat-clutching, eye-stinging haze gave the furnacelike kitchen a crepuscular aspect.

This was the only remaining room and the thirteen men crammed into it and began to load their weapons for the last time. All except McSween. The vital force that sustains every mortal through hardship, impelling him to action, had dwindled out of the lawyer's libido. He sat slumped in a corner in an abject state of collapse.

Billy felt responsible for the apathetic man. He wanted to try to get him out of the house alive, somehow. Assuming a cheerful attitude he attempted to give McSween a loaded Colt.

"Here you go, governor," he said. "Let's go out fighting."

McSween refused the weapon, murmuring, "God will look out for me."

Could be, but Billy preferred to put his trust in a six-shooter.

"We'll go out in small groups," he told his friends. "Run out one at a time—don't jam up in the door. Try to get through the gate in the plank fence on your right, and run like hades for the river. Morris, Zamora, and Romero will go first and break trail for McSween. Then Doc, French, Salazar, Gonzalez, and the two Chavez boys. Davis, Tom, and me will go last."

He peered through one of the shuttered windows at the sky. There was a speckle of stars but no moon. That was good; but the angry red glow cast by the flames wasn't going to be any help at all.

It was what Dolan's men were counting on.

Under cover of darkness Kinney's boys closed in on the burning house. Along with a handful of Seven Rivers men they edged up toward the back of the stable and the rear adobe wall. The gunfire had slacked off. A warm wind brewed up from the mesa and struck the hot, pungent, choking volumes of smoke and wafted it eastward.

McSween's ruined home stood out like a great bonfire in the midst of a black abyss. Most of it was now smoldering embers. Only the one fiery boxlike room remained. The kitchen door faced the back yard. In a moment thirteen desperate men would have to make their bid for freedom through that door—across thirty feet of illuminated yard, through the side fence or over the rear wall, and down to the Bonito that gurgled musically in the dark.

Twenty tense men trained their rifles on the distant door.

Billy eased open the kitchen door and took a peek outside. An undulating coil of smoke spread a hazy smear over the yard. Time to hit the trail. He threw the door wide open.

"Váyanse, amigos!"

Morris, Zamora, and Romero sprang into the yard and hit running. The Kinney rifles jolted furiously and the winging slugs tumbled Vincente Romero and Francisco Zamora headlong to the fire-flickering ground. Harvey Morris went racing toward the plank fence, bent double, but a second Winchester burst sent him sprawling by the gate post.

Now was the time—before they could reload! Billy threw open the door again, yelling "Now! Now!" at McSween, and the unarmed lawyer lurched into the flame-fluttering yard.

He moved like a man in a dream, not seeming to know where he was going or what he was going to do. Confusedly he turned toward the rear adobe wall instead of running to the east fence. As he stumbled toward the chicken house against the adobe wall, he called out:

"I am McSween! I surrender!"

Young Bob Beckwith was crouching just behind the henhouse with five other Dolanites, and he suddenly stepped into the gateway in the adobe wall. Whether he intended to shoot McSween or take him prisoner has never been established. Half a dozen hidden rifles abruptly sliced lead at the stumbling lawyer and Alexander McSween went down in a lifeless heap with five bullets in his body.

Legend has it that Beckwith then yelled, "I got McSween!"

A dozen voices whooped with delight. In that same instant Billy flung open the door for the third time.

"Vamos, hombres!"

Six men burst from the house, coming one two

three, one two three. The uproar from Kinney's rifles was deafening. Hijinio Salazar went down with two slugs in his hide. Ignacio Gonzales stumbled, clutched at his shattered arm, and ran on. Chavez y Chavez was nicked but didn't stop to worry about it, staying close on the tail of Florencio Chavez who was following Doc Scurlock.

Tough old Doc swerved away from both gates and took the middle course just to the right of the outhouse. He hit the corner where the adobe wall joined the plank fence, rolled over the wall on his gut, and disappeared into the clamorous dark. The two Chavez boys came right after him.

At the same time Jim French headed straight for the fence gate, paused for a moment to make a grab at the sprawled Harvey Morris, changed his mind and ran on toward Tunstall's corral, zagging to the left to reach the Bonito. The wounded Gonzales tailed him like a scampering shadow.

Unseen by anyone, Charlie Bowdre, George Coe, and Hendry Brown chose that chaotic moment to make their getaway from the store. They raced across the smoke-strung corral, rolled the rear wall and ran down into the dark arroyo. Home free!

Billy gave a triumphant yell. Five out of six had made it to safety that time. That was the way to go! The door flew open and Jim Davis hit the yard like a scared jack rabbit, all humped over and heel-churning the dust. He was gone!

Tom and Billy exchanged a flashing grin, and then Tom sprang through the doorway, blasting with his Colt like a crazy man, and got so bollixed up out there that Billy didn't see how the lanky Texas boy could possibly make it.

Orange streaks of flame spurted from the black curtain of night as Kinney's rifles crackled vindictively. One of the slugs clipped Tom's right shoulder and spun him halfway around, knocking the Colt from his stunned hand. Regaining his equilibrium, he jumped over Salazar's body and started to run again but stopped short when he realized he was running smack toward the adobe wall! He cut to the right with bullets snipping the air around him and made it to the gate where he slid to a halt and snatched at Morris. The youth was already dead so he dropped him, and then was through the gate and long-legging it for the Bonito.

Billy shouted. Good old Tom! Now it was his turn to lay some tracks. He was the last to leave the burning house to make the horrific dash to safety. A branch of flame forked through a hole in the roof and the interior of the room became lit up with the fluctuating glare. He drew and cocked two six-shooters.

The Dolan men leveled their rifles at the burning kitchen. McSween was through; now there was only this last man—the one *hombre* they really wanted—the eighteen-year-old cowboy who had baffled and eluded and outfought them for five hectic months.

A shadow moved—a thin silhouette leaped into the glowing doorway.

"It's the Kid!" a dozen voices cried, and the stabbing yellow fingers from twenty rifles jabbed at him.

He ran through the leaden holocaust with death snapping viciously at his heels. Ducking, twisting, nothing seemed to touch him. Dolan's crowd had been too eager; they were guilty of mass reflex fire—jerking their triggers with buck fever. Billy had a Colt in each hand and his small clenched fists exploded as he went across the yard in a running crouch.

Bob Beckwith, just inside the wall, caught a slug spang in the head and slumped down beside Mc-Sween. Another man, Ben Litchfield, jumped back from the wall with his mouth and left eye torn open. Winchesters churned the dirt around Billy but he seemed to be running under a charm. He leaped over Zamora, over Romero, dodged through the fence gate and headed for Tunstall's store, thinking that Bowdre, Coe, and Brown were still holed up in there.

Three Negro troopers were lurking at the rear of the store and they raised their carbines as they saw the Kid zigzagging toward them. Instantly Billy spotted a glitter of firelight on their barrels and he ducked, swerved to the left and took off for the Bonito with the troopers' bullets humming on ahead of him.

In darkness now he went plunging and sliding down the shaly, shelving riverbed, stumbled and thrashed across the chattering Bonito and crawled into the black thickets on the other side. He dropped in his tracks, totally exhausted.

"Billy?" Tom's voice whispered in the stygian willows.

Billy got up and pushed through the thicket until he came upon his fatigued and battered *compadres*. His spunk was restored when he saw how many of them were there. True, they had lost McSween; but the best of the old bunch—Tom, Doc, French, Bowdre, Middleton, Waite, Brown, and the two Coes—were still alive and kicking. Dolan and Peppin hadn't put such a dent in them after all. It could have been a lot worse.

Fred Waite said all the horses were back in a nearby draw, so Billy and his little band set out for San Patricio. The Regulators' *noche triste*, sad night, was over.

Chapter 9

The fifteen-year-old boy Hijinio Salazar lay face down in McSween's backyard only a dozen feet from the burning kitchen. He had been drilled in the left shoulder and left hip and his hand had been creased. He was still alive.

Some twenty feet to his right lay the crumpled bodies of McSween and Beckwith. A little distance beyond his sprawled boots were the two dead Mexicans Romero and Zamora. Harvey Morris was slumped by the fence. All the others were gone.

The young boy listened to the victory shouts of Dolan's men as they came trotting into the yard. He closed his eyes and laid very still, hardly daring to breathe, feigning death in the hope that he would be overlooked by his enemies.

His wounds were extremely painful, yet his loss of blood was slowly lulling him into sleep. *Don't pass out, Hijinio!* he warned himself. His unconscious breathing would be too labored, would call attention to the fact that he was still alive. He concentrated on staying awake, on playing possum.

The smoky yard was illuminated by the cheery

glow of the crackling fire as the Kinney and Dolan men came in to inspect the results of the battle. Salazar held his breath. The men were arguing now as to who had hit which man, and a whiskey bottle was moving from hand to hand.

There is a well-worn legend that they held a drunken revel in the red glare of the flames, singing and dancing around the bodies of their dead foes. It is not true. They went away in a little while, all except Andy Boyle and a deputy named Pierce who stayed to poke among the corpses. They used their rifle barrels as pokers.

Boyle paused over Salazar with a suspicious look in his boozy eyes. Was that *muchacho* dead or just playing at it? He gave the boy a couple of testing kicks in the ribs, then got him by the back of his gunbelt and bounced him up and down a few times.

Salazar clenched his jaw and let the rest of himself go as limp as a rag, determined not to move a muscle or make a sound no matter how great the pain. Boyle planted the muzzle of his rifle against the boy's ear.

"I think this greaser kid is still alive," he said.

Deputy Pierce glanced at Salazar and shook his head.

"He's dead enough," he said. "Don't waste a bullet on him. Speaking of kids—it's too bad we didn't pick off Kid Antrim. That boy is as hard to catch as a flea on a fox."

The two men moved off, chattering like a pair of magpies. The boy expelled his breath. A moment later his brain whirled and he passed out. The fire had dwindled into a glowing bed of embers when he became conscious again. He had a feeling that dawn was not far off. Forcing himself to his hands and knees he painfully crawled away from the prone bodies in the silent yard.

He reached the Bonito and took a long drink, then

dragged himself along the riverbed to his sister-in-law's house. The poor woman thought he was a ghost! She had been told earlier that he was dead. Unobtrusively she slipped into the cavalry camp and found Surgeon Appel who returned with her to tend Salazar's wounds.

The fifteen-year-old boy who had successfully shammed death was destined to outlive nearly everyone concerned in the Lincoln County War. He died on January 7, 1936. The epitaph on his grave reads: A pal of Billy the Kid.

In those bleak July days following the disastrous showdown in Lincoln, Billy needed all the pals he could get. He was suddenly running short of them. The Mexican-Americans had already given the feud up as a bad job and returned to their farms and families; Jim French, mistrusting the temper of the times, lit out on his own; Frank and George Coe had gone back to their ranches on the Ruidoso; and Charlie Bowdre and Doc Scurlock wanted to return home to their Mexican wives and try to forget their lost cause.

Billy had no wife or family or home to go to. The closest he had ever come to putting down roots had been there in turbulent Lincoln County, and it went against his grain to be forced out by the likes of Dolan and Peppin. But Fred Waite and Middleton suggested they do just that—vamoose out of the Territory while the getting was good.

Billy couldn't see it. Just because they had lost a battle didn't mean they had lost the war. He believed they had fought on the right side, and he figured they should hang around to see if they couldn't do a little good somehow.

So it was agreed. They would stick together a little longer and see what developed. The first thing they wanted to do was find out what had become of

Tunstall's 400 head of cattle. Hearing that the herd had been driven to a ranch west of White Sands they started in that direction, heading southwest through the Mescalero Apache Reservation. George Coe accompanied them on this expedition.

On August 5 Fred Godfrey and Morris Bernstein, both clerks in the Indian agency, heard that a large band of Regulators was passing through the reservation. Bernstein, with more courage than prudence, grabbed a rifle and a horse and went galloping down the arroyo to find the outlaws. Five Apaches followed him.

It wasn't Billy's band. It was ex-Constable Martinez with a party of San Patricio Mexicans. They too were out looking for Tunstall's stolen herd, and had just stopped at the creek below the agency to water their horses.

Bernstein suddenly burst into sight and started shooting like a madman. Riding headlong for Martinez, he snapped two wild shots and the ex-constable jumped behind a tree and drew his pistol. Bernstein spurred his horse toward the tree and fired again. This time Martinez fired back and Bernstein hit the ground dead.

Billy and his pals were nearly half a mile away when they heard the shooting, and they galloped for the deep timber. Without warning, Apache bullets whizzed by them like hailstones so they hunkered in their saddles and wheeled toward the creek, where they ran into the excited Mexicans.

"What's all the shooting about?" Coe yelled.

"Some *loco gringo* attacked us with Indians and we shot him!"

And that was absolutely all the Regulators knew of the affair. Agent Fred Godfrey, however, completely misinterpreted the facts and telegraphed the following message to Fort Stanton:

Morris J. Bernstein my clerk was brutally murdered today by McSween outlaws . . .

What more could Dudley and Peppin ask for? They quickly drafted an erroneous report charging that William Bonney, Tom O'Folliard, Fred Waite, Hendry Brown, John Middleton, Charlie Bowdre, George Coe, Doc Scurlock, and Jim French had murdered Bernstein (even though Doc, French and Bowdre were no longer with Billy!) and sent it to Governor Axtell.

Federal warrants were promptly issued against all of the Regulators *who had not even been at the scene of the shooting*, but Martinez was never indicted. At a later date all of these absurd indictments were canceled—except for the one against William Bonney.

That was the way it went from then on. If a brawling cowboy was shot at El Paso, Texas, Billy the Kid was named as the gunslinger. If a stage was robbed near the Arizona border, Billy the Kid was undoubtedly the holdup man. If a horse was stolen from Santa Fe in the north or a few head of cattle from the Pecos region in the east, who else but Billy the Kid could be the rustler?

The Lincoln County War had caused great enmity and bitterness in both high and low circles. Someone had to be saddled with the blame for all the bloodshed and hatred, and it seemed to be almost unanimously agreed that that someone should be Billy the Kid.

Bolstered by the authority of federal warrants, Colonel Dudley happily sent out a detachment of troopers to track down the remaining Regulators. In the meantime Kinney's outlaws—under the pretense of looking for Billy the Kid—rode roughshod over the hapless county, raiding isolated farms, stealing horses, rustling everything that had horns and hoofs. Neither the army nor the law made any attempt to stop these depredations against peaceful citizens.

Sheriff Peppin, in fact, was not making much of an attempt at anything. A noticeable change had occurred in Dad since that fateful Friday night of July 19. He seemed to lack his old get-up-and-go, becoming more and more reticent, as if he intended to passively retire from the scene.

A change had come over the firebrand Jimmy Dolan too. Most of his riders had deserted him, he no longer had any control over Kinney's crowd, his old booze-soaked partner Major Murphy had died in Santa Fe, and the protracted feud had put a drastic dent in The House's financial stability. Murphy & Co. was stumbling toward bankruptcy.

Billy and his little band had no chance to contemplate these changes in Lincoln; they were busy keeping on the dodge from Dudley's troopers and Kinney's marauders. They crossed the Hondo late in August and headed for Chisum's ranch. It would make a safe hideout for a while, and there was also a debt to be settled.

The Regulators had been acting in the interest of the Chisum-McSween-Tunstall combine for six arduous months and had never received a dime for their efforts. They didn't expect anything from Mrs. McSween or Tunstall's heirs, but old Uncle John was a rich man and it was time he shelled out some of it.

Wily Uncle John thought otherwise. Had he personally *asked* the Regulators to fight his battle for him? Had he ever made *any* agreement with them, verbal or on paper? If they wanted to ride around the county and get into gunfights that was their business, not his. As far as he was concerned he didn't owe them a plugged nickle.

Legend says that Billy then declared he was placing Uncle John's name at the head of his list of men he intended to kill. This has never been authenticated. It is far more likely that he and Tom, Fred Waite, Hendry Brown, and Middleton simply went out and rounded up a sizeable herd of Chisum's cattle and drove them off to the nearest market, merely to square their account with the penurious old rancher.

In any event, Uncle John lost no time in accusing Billy of rustling his stock and even offered a reward for his capture. Some thanks for six months of hard riding and fighting.

Conceding that Billy and his boys took the cattle, the handiest market would have been old Fort Sumner located on a cottonwood-circled bench of the Rio Pecos, thirty-some miles north of Chisum's cow camp at Bosque Grande.

Sumner was an old army outpost built by the Yankees in the Civil War and since abandoned. Old Lucien Maxwell, a famous sheep and cattleman, had bought the fort in 1874 and moved his Mexican family, his peons, and lock, stock, and barrel into the empty barracks. He died in 1875, leaving everything in the hands of his son Pedro "Pete" Maxwell.

Billy and his *compadres* arrived at the sprawling fort sometime in September and immediately made friends with Pete Maxwell, as well as with all of Sumner's Mexican-American inhabitants. It was at this time that the Regulators met a man who was to have the final say in the last chapter of the saga of Billy the Kid.

He was a rawboned quiet man of twenty-eight. Standing six foot four, he sported the popular handlebar mustache and he hailed—among other places —from Texas. He had killed a buffalo hunter in self-defense in West Texas in 1877, and had turned himself in to a justice of the peace. There was no warrant out for him, and exactly why he had rambled into New Mexico was not known. Now he was the bartender in Beaver Smith's Fort Sumner saloon.

His name was Patrick Floyd Garrett.

The Regulators shook his hand over the bar and a spontaneous liking kindled between the tall morose Texan and the young buoyant outlaw. As different as a grizzly and a lobo a mutual attraction existed between Billy and Pat that was hard to define; about the only thing they had in common was a love for cards, which they indulged in day after day.

Gambling, horse-racing, attending Mexican fiestas and fandangos, the Regulators passed contentedly through a rare month of peace. Then it was time to take to the trail again. Word had reached them that Doc and Charlie wanted to move up to Fort Sumner, and Billy was determined to return to Lincoln to give his old pards safe conduct.

There is a belief that Billy and the others quietly slipped into Mrs. McSween's new home (Baca's old house by the Torreon) one dark night to get the latest news. This much is certain—they soon learned that Susan McSween was doing everything in her power to ruin Colonel Dudley: primarily through wrathful denunciations which reached as far as the White House some 1,600 miles away.

She had found the support of a one-armed hotheaded lawyer named Huston Chapman and this rabid legal-beagle was kicking up an awful stink in Lincoln County, charging everyone from the lowly gunman Jesse Evans to the exaulted Colonel Dudley with the most heinous crimes imaginable.

One other vital bit of information the Regulators picked up during their brief visit to Lincoln: Frank Angel's investigation of the bloody vendetta was beginning to pay off. Acting on Angel's information, President Hayes had seen fit to remove Governor Axtell from office and Lew Wallace, the famous author-general, had been appointed governor of New Mexico Territory. He had also been handed the appalling job of trying to legally untangle the hopelessly interwoven causes and results of the Lincoln County War.

What this amounted to was that the luckless Wallace (who was trying to write his classic novel *Ben Hur* in his spare time) had to investigate and dissect all the rumors, accusations, sworn statements, indictments and warrants that had been floating around ever since the Mesilla court had issued the first writ of attachment against McSween's property.

Consider the ensuing complications . . .

Sheriff Brady had legally deputized Bill Morton's posse (excepting Jesse Evans' banditti) and given them an illegal writ against Tunstall. In the performance of their duty they had killed Tunstall (no warrant against him) and fired on U.S. Deputy Marshal Bob Widenmann. Where did that leave Morton's posse? Had they committed justifiable homicide, as they claimed, or were they guilty of murder? And was Brady blameless or not?

Justice Wilson had ruled it murder and had appointed Dick Brewer special constable and deputized the Regulators to serve warrants on Tunstall's killers, and they, in accordance, had killed deputies Morton, Roberts, and Hindman as well as undeputized Baker and Sheriff Brady for whom there was no warrant. In retaliation Deputy Sheriff Peppin's posse (legally deputized?) had killed Deputy McNab (no warrant against him) and taken Deputy Coe a prisoner, only to have the special constable's posse (mere vigilantes?) shoot Deputy (?) Campbell in the leg. And who, by the way, was responsible for Deputy McCloskey's death?

And so it went—charge and countercharge, until the entire mess made as much sense as a hurrah's nest. And there seemed to be no end to it because it was still going on in what has been called the Aftermath. Morris Bernstein's death appeared to have bearing on the feud; reputedly Ignacio Gonzales had died from the wound he had received on the night of July 19; and late in September four pro-McSween Mexican boys by the name of Sanches were gunned down by either Kinney's raiders or some of Dolan's old Seven Rivers riders.

It is no wonder that the newly-appointed governor, having stepped unwittingly into this bewildering muddle, soon threw his hands in the air and declared his famous Amnesty Proclamation.

In the interim Billy and his pards had helped Doc Scurlock and Charlie Bowdre move their wives and possessions through the Capitan Gap and north across the windblown mesa to Fort Sumner.

Doc was definitely through with the feud and he settled down to go to work for Pete Maxwell. Charlie Bowdre followed his lead but it was pretty apparent that he missed the wild old days of hoofing it along the back trails and holding gun skirmishes with Dolan's crowd wherever they happened to cross paths. This yen for excitement ultimately proved to be his downfall.

It was mid-November when Billy first read Lew Wallace's Amnesty Proclamation, which was intended to restore peace and harmony to the vendetta-stricken county. It read in part:

> The undersigned (Wallace) . . . proclaims a general pardon for misdemeanors and offenses committed in the said County of Lincoln against the laws of the Territory, between the first day of February, 1878, and the date of this proclamation. It shall not apply . . .(to) any person in bar of conviction under indictment now found and returned for any such crimes or misdemeanors.

The proclamation was a godsend to many of the gunfighters who had participated in the war and who had not yet been indicted, but it didn't do a thing for any of those who were under indictment. Many of the original warrants which had been issued from the time of Tunstall's death in February to the time of Bernstein's death in August had been pigeonholed and forgotten or simply dropped. But every warrant against Billy the Kid was still in force. He was now wanted for the murders of Morton, Baker, Brady, Hindman, Roberts, Beckwith, and Bernstein.

He didn't understand why he had to assume the entire blame for the Lincoln County imbroglio. Now nearly every *gringo* in the Territory was his enemy, inasmuch as any man could declare himself a bounty hunter and shoot him on sight in order to claim the various rewards that had been posted on him.

It was enough for Fred Waite, John Middleton, and Hendry Brown. They had tried to fight for justice and had ended up with the whole territory down on them. It was time to cash in and pull out. Middleton and Brown decided to light out for Kansas. Waite said he was going to seek sanctuary in the Cherokee Indian Nation. He thought the world of Billy and begged the boy to come with him.

No. Alone and with everything going against him, Billy was determined not to give up. To run away acknowledged guilt and defeat, neither of which he felt. He would hang on till the final showdown. But he was not quite alone. Tom O'Folliard grinned and said he would stick too. Billy was his lodestar.

The five *compadres* shook hands for the last time. Then three of them mounted up and headed north. Billy and Tom, the two stormy petrels, turned their ponies south and started plodding down the long, lonesome trail to Lincoln. Billy had just turned nineteen.

Chapter 10

Dad Peppin, haunted by the fear that one of his many enemies would drygulch him some dark night, turned in his badge and quietly withdrew from the turbulent scene. Governor Wallace appointed a non-partial man by the name of George Kimbrell as the new sheriff.

That was in December, and late in January Billy and Tom were hanging around the outskirts of Lincoln, sending out feelers to see if they could get a pardon under the Amnesty Proclamation. The new sheriff seemed friendly toward the two boys, and Mrs. McSween's lawyer, Chapman, was willing to help them in any way he could. He even wrote an appeal to Tunstall's father in England, requesting funds for the remaining Regulators:

> They were promised by both McSween and Widenmann that they would receive pay for hunting down the murderers of your son, but they do not ask any pay, but think that something should be done to assist them out of their present trouble, as it would be a vindication of your son. If you can do anything for them, I think that they

deserve it. They have been indicted for the killing of some of the murderers of your son, and are without means of defending themselves . . .

There was no response to Chapman's letter.

The situation in Lincoln had Jimmy Dolan on tenterhooks. His old yes-man Peppin was gone, his ally Colonel Dudley was in hot water up to his neck with the governor, and now Mrs. McSween and Chapman were doing their utmost to drag him into court and bring about his ultimate ruin. In desperation Dolan hit upon the crafty idea of burying the hatchet with Billy the Kid. If they could come to a private agreement, perhaps Billy wouldn't testify against him. It would be a case of "You scratch my back, I scratch yours."

It might have been the bizarreness of the situation that appealed to Billy and Tom, or maybe they thought it would be the first step toward seeking a Territorial pardon. In any event they rode into town on February 18, 1879—exactly one year after Tunstall's death—and pulled up before Stockton's saloon.

Dolan, Mathews, Jesse Evans, Bill Campbell, and three nameless gunhands were waiting for them in the bar. Campbell, still limping from the shot he had received from George Coe, was half drunk and in a surly mood. But the boisterous greeting Dolan and Jesse gave their two old enemies seemed sincere enough. Dolan was especially eager that all hands should stop beating the war drum and make peace.

It is not known exactly what transpired during this strange pow-wow, but according to various accounts Dolan, Mathews, and Campbell became belligerently drunk, while Billy, Tom, and Jesse did very little drinking and tried to maintain a sense of camaraderie. The "peace" talk broke up shortly before ten p.m. and the nine men went out into the dark street to go their separate ways.

They bumped smack into the one-armed lawyer Huston Chapman. Bill Campbell immediately lurched forward aggressively.

"Where do you think you're going, lawyer?" he growled.

"I'm going about my own business which is no concern of yours," the fearless lawyer snapped back.

"You better change your tone, *hombre*," Campbell snarled, "or I might change it for you."

Sensing that violence was about to pop, and not wanting any part of it, Billy started to back off. A pistol barrel was planted in his side and he heard Jesse hiss, "Don't make a move, Billy."

Glancing to the right Billy saw that Mathews was holding a gun on Tom. All the rest of the drunken men were poised to draw and blast. It wasn't the time to make a wrong move—maybe Jesse was trying to keep him from getting drilled. Seven against two were bad odds. Billy and Tom remained very still.

"You can't scare me," Chapman said stiffly. "I know your kind and it's no use. You've tried that before."

"Then I'll settle you proper this time!" Campbell cried, and he hooked out his Colt and the pistol jumped with a flashing *blam*!

Lawyer Chapman pitched over backwards with a bullet through his chest. Dolan fired at the downed man, and then the rest of the drunken brutes surged forward yelling and waving their pistols. Someone poured whiskey on the lawyer's body; someone else struck a match to it.

Sickened by this senseless and barbaric act, Billy looked quickly around and saw that no one except Jesse was watching him and Tom now. It's quite likely that even Jesse was appalled by the gruesome scene. He offered no resistance when Billy and Tom turned away and walked hurriedly toward the corral.

That was the end of the strange relationship between Billy the Kid and Jesse Evans. They never saw each other again.

Billy and Tom took to the hills and stayed there for three weeks. They had good reason to believe that they would be implicated in the murder simply because nearly every crime committed in Lincoln County was automatically pinned on Billy and his *compadres*. It was early March when they deemed it safe enough to venture into San Patricio to pick up the current news.

Colonel Dudley, they learned, had finally made a mistake that Governor Wallace could use as a legal club. Dudley, knowing full well that Dolan, Campbell, Mathews, and Evans had murdered Chapman, had blithely let them go free. Wallace, through the sanction of General Hatch USA, had Dudley relieved a command pending a court of inquiry which would investigate the colonel's dubious methods. The governor then had the four murderers arrested and placed under guard at Fort Stanton.

And sure enough—Wallace had also offered $1,000 reward for the capture of Billy the Kid as an accessory to Chapman's murder.

Sick and tired of having to bear the blame for every man who was shot in New Mexico, Billy wrote a letter to Wallace explaining that he had gone to Lincoln to discuss a truce with Dolan and Evans, that he had been an unwilling witness of the murder, and would readily testify against the murderers if it were not for the numerous indictments hanging over his head. If Wallace would annul those indictments, he would surrender himself as a Territorial witness. One of the statements in his letter shows a certain wistfullness that is rather touching:

"I have no wish to fight any more . . ."

On March 15 he received an urgent letter from the governor:

Come to the house of old Squire Wilson at nine o'clock next Monday night alone . . .I have authority to exempt you from prosecution, if you will testify to what you say you know . . .The utmost secrecy is to be used. So come alone. Don't tell anybody—not a living soul—where you are coming or the object. If you could trust Jesse Evans, you can trust me.

The governor's word was good enough for Billy. Promptly at nine o'clock, March 17, he knocked on the back door of Squire Wilson's home. Wilson let him in.

"I was sent for to meet the Governor," Billy said. "Is he here?"

A scarecrow of a man with a tufty goatee came toward the nineteen-year-old outlaw, saying, "I am Governor Wallace."

Billy, holding his Winchester, looked around cautiously.

"Your note promised absolute protection," he said.

"And I have been true to my promise. Squire Wilson and I are the only men in the house."

The outlaw and the governor got down to business.

"If you will testify before the court of inquiry and at the trial against the murderers of Chapman, I will let you go scot-free with a pardon in your pocket for all your misdeeds."

Billy was willing to earn his pardon, but not at the risk of catching a bullet in the back.

"Governor, they would kill me if I were to do what you ask. I'd never get out of town alive."

"We can prevent that," Wallace said. "You will consent to a prearranged arrest, so that your capture will appear to be genuine. In that manner your enemies will not realize that you have been brought in as a Territorial witness."

It was agreed and they mapped out the arrangements for Billy's so-called capture. Billy made certain stipulations: Sheriff Kimbrell would have to make the arrest with a hand-picked posse comprised of Mexican-Americans. Under no conditions would any Fort Stanton soldiers be included. He would as soon trust his life with someone like John Kinney as with one of Dudley's troopers.

The meeting was concluded and Billy and Wallace shook hands and parted as friends. The boy outlaw kept his word. The governor did not.

Four days later, March 21, the sheriff's posse rode into San Patricio and took Billy and Tom into custody. There was no trouble about the "arrest" and the prisoners were escorted back to Lincoln. Everything went off as planned until Billy and Tom were conducted to the dingy little jailhouse which was actually a dungeonlike cellar with a shanty built over it.

At that point Billy suddenly balked. He had agreed to an informal confinement; Wallace had said nothing about locking them up in the rat-haunted town jail. According to Ash Upson, Billy turned to Deputy Sheriff Tom Longworth and said:

"Tom, I've sworn I would never go inside that hole alive."

"I don't see how you or I can help it, Billy," Longworth said. "I don't want to put you there, but that's orders and I have to carry 'em out. You don't want to make trouble for me, do you?"

No, Billy didn't—and he and Tom O'Folliard tramped down the steps to their subterranean cell. This was the first indication Billy had that the governor was content to use him as a mere tool rather than as a trusted friend. He didn't understand that kind of play. It went against the code he and Tom believed in.

Inexplicably, the two young outlaws were moved to a room in the back of Patron's building the next day. Handcuffs were clamped to their wrists but these had little effect on Billy. He passed the time-heavy hours amusing Tom by showing him how easily he could shuck off the cuffs over his small hands.

The trial against Chapman's murderers was scheduled for the second week in April, but Campbell and Jesse Evans (with the help of a U.S. trooper!) made an escape from Fort Stanton late in March and disappeared forever from the Lincoln County scene.

Come April Billy appeared at court and gave testimony against Chapman's murderers, but it was a waste of time. Dolan and Mathews had been indicted as accessories in the crime and the prosecuting attorney was none other than Colonel Rynerson, their old Santa Fe Ring pal. Rynerson got them a change of venue to Socorro County where they had no trouble securing a dismissal on their case.

With even less effort Rynerson saw to it that all of the Seven Rivers men who had been indicted for the murder of Frank McNab were released under the governor's amnesty.

Then came the stunner. Rynerson turned his judicial gunsights on Billy the Kid. True, most of the indictments against him had been dropped, but Wallace had been unable to quash the indictment for the murder of Sheriff Brady. This was Rynerson's ace in the hole and he was determined to make the most of it. He asked Judge Bristol for a change of venue and the judge quickly granted it.

The trial was scheduled for a later date and the place was designated as Mesilla, which was Rynerson's home base. Billy could easily see that Rynerson intended to hand pick a jury that would "railroad" him straight to the gallows. And no doubt the presiding judge would be Bristol.

Tom could read the prophetic handwriting on the wall as easily as Billy. The governor had let them down and it was high time to make a break for it. You only danced once on the end of a rope and Tom had no intention of making that final fandango.

Neither did Billy—but he wasn't ready to cut and run. He had promised to testify at the court of inquiry concerning Dudley's conduct in the Four Days' Battle, and he would live up to his bargain. Anyhow, why work up a lather about it so soon? His Mesilla trial was not scheduled until July, and by that time he planned to be long gone.

The court of inquiry opened late in May. It took place at Fort Stanton and was comprised of three high-ranking army officers. Billy took the oath on May 28.

"What is your name and place of resident?"

"My name is William Bonney. I reside in Lincoln."

"Are you known or called Billy Kid? Also Kid Antrim?"

"Yes sir, though Antrim's my stepfather's name."

"Where were you on the 19th of July last, and what, if anything did you see of the movements and actions of the troops that day?"

He was heavily qustioned by the court, and then cross-examined by Colonel Dudley. Throughout the entire time he was on the stand he was as cool and straight-faced as if he were playing poker. Only he, Mrs. McSween, and Jose Chavez y Chavez were there to testify against Dudley. Both men testified that the troopers had fired at them, and Mrs. McSween gave a detailed account of Dudley's callous indifference regarding the men trapped in her burning home.

The three officers reached a decision in mid-June.

Colonel Dudley was innocent! Furthermore, they found that he had acted with "the most humane and worthy motives and of good military judgment under exceptional circumstances."

It was too much for Billy. This last sample of Territorial justice was more than he could swallow. From now on he would rely solely upon his horse, Colt, and wits. That night he and Tom slipped out of the Patron house and walked over to the Ellis corral, mounted their ponies and rode off into the dark mesa.

It was the night of June 17, 1879. Tom O'Folliard had exactly eighteen months to live. Billy the Kid had twenty-five.

The next year was a lazy one for the two young outlaws. Much of their time was spent at Fort Sumner—playing poker with Pat Garrett, squiring young senoritas to the local *bailes* (dances), and horse racing with anyone who was willing to take them on.

When the cards went against them and they felt the pressure for some fresh pocket money, they would ramble down toward Bosque Grande and pay a moonlight visit on Uncle John's grazing herd. *Por qué no*? Why not? He still owed them money. Besides, it was a good joke on the old miser.

But Chisum didn't think it was a bit funny. In his anger he brought pressure to bear on certain political bigwigs to bring about the appointment of a new sheriff—some fearless and ambitious man who would not hesitate to rid the Territory of Billy the Kid once and for all. As chance would have it there just happened to be a fearless and highly ambitious man in New Mexico at that time. It was Pat Garrett.

Another man who aspired after greatness rode into Fort Sumner in January of 1880. His name was Joe

Grant, a young obnoxious braggart from Texas. His lofty ambition was to kill Billy the Kid and make a name for himself. But first he had to rib up his nerve through whisky.

Billy dropped into Hargrove's saloon one night and saw Grant slouching over a bottle at the bar. He didn't think anything about the man until the bartender whispered a warning that Grant had been boasting how he intend to "kill the Kid" at the first opportunity. Traditionally, this is the scene that ensued:

Grant swaggered down to Billy's end of the bar and said, "Kid, I'll bet I kill a man tonight before you do."

"You got the wrong pig by the ear," Billy said. "I don't want to kill anybody." Quite casually he reached for Grant's pistol, saying, "That's a nice looking Colt. Mind if I have a look?"

Pretending to admire the inlaid barrel, he noticed there were only five cartridges in Grant's six-shooter and, as he returned the Colt to the Texan's holster, he thumbed the cylinder so that when the hammer was cocked the empty chamber would roll into firing position.

Before long Grant got completely out of hand. Barging behind the bar he began to smash the glasses and bottles with his pistol barrel. Billy watched the drunken fool with narrowed eyes. Suddenly Grant swung about and aimed his Colt in Billy's face.

"I'm collecting that bet now!" he yelled.

He squeezed the trigger and the firing pin clicked in the empty chamber. Blinking his surprise, he started to cock the hammer for another try. It was his last move. Billy's pistol leaped in his hand and Joe Grant dropped dead where he was standing.

Billy holstered his pistol and shook his head. It was obviously self-defense but he imagined the law would put a different name on it. His only comment on the incident was, "It was a game for two—and I got there first."

That summer a noticeable rift began to widen between Billy and his card-playing pal Pat Garrett. More and more now Pat was chumming with Chisum and some other powerful ranchers. When they started to pull the strings to have him made deputy sheriff, he saw fit to go into business with them and he moved down to Roswell to start his own small ranch.

It seemed to Billy that Pat was set on becoming Chisum's tool in order to feather his own nest. The next thing he and Tom knew their erstwhile friends would be coming after them with warrants and a posse. That kind of friendship was *muy loco* to them.

Doc Scurlock didn't like the way things were shaping up in the Territory and decided to pull out of New Mexico for good. Charlie Bowdre should have gone, but he had landed a cushy foreman job on a ranch not far from Sumner and didn't want to give it up. So Billy said *adios* to Doc for the last time and the one-time dentist, rancher, and gunfighter struck out for Texas with his Mexican wife.

Billy and Tom started to cast around for some new *compadres* and the three men who joined them were an odd mixture of good and bad.

The first was a cheerful teenager called Billie Wilson who had a bad habit of paying his way with counterfeit money. The second was a former peace officer named Tom Pickett who had gotten into some kind of scrape in Las Vegas. And the third was a thorough badman, a dangerous character named Dave Rudabaugh, who was wanted for a long and varied list of crimes. These men naturally gravitated toward Billy, automatically accepting him as their

116

leader.

It was a far cry from the old Regulator band, but at least it gave Billy and Tom a sense of support. And they needed it . . .

In November of 1880 Pat Garrett ran for the office of Lincoln County sheriff and won the election. His primary duty, as described to him by Chisum and the other big ranchers, was quite plain. As soon as he pinned on his tin star, he was to set out and get Billy the Kid—dead or alive.

Chapter 11

Winter was sending crisp winds over the flat mesas and table-top hills and Billy and his little band shifted with the free-blowing currents, as elusive as a will-o'-the-wisp, keeping always one good jump ahead of Sheriff Garrett's hard-riding posse.

It wouldn't do Billy any good to leave the Territory because on top of being sheriff, Garrett had also been appointed Deputy U.S. Marshal which gave him the authority to make an arrest in any town, county, territory, or state. He was spreading himself thick in his mad chase after his one-time friend.

To add insult to injury one of Billy's worst enemies, Bob Olinger, was a deputy in Garrett's posse. The private feud between Billy the Kid and Bob Olinger has become a classic tale. Billy believed that Olinger had killed his *compadre* Frank McNab, and Olinger believed that Billy had killed his best friend Bob Beckwith. They thoroughly hated one another.

Six days after his twenty-first birthday Billy pulled into the little town of White Oaks, forty miles northwest of Lincoln. His purpose in going there was to look up his friend Judge Leonard, who had served as Governor Wallace's assistant in the Lincoln trial, to learn if Wallace had made any move yet to eliminate the indictment that was still hanging over him for the murder of Sheriff Brady.

He had no opportunity to see the judge. Learning of his arrival a group of White Oaks citizens hastily formed a vigilante group to capture or kill the infamous Billy the Kid. Billy and his boys made a wild gallop down the main street and barely got out of town by the skin of their teeth, with Billy taking a parting shot at one of the vigilantes, which he later described as "only a friendly shot."

Early the next day the vigilantes jumped the outlaws while they were making breakfast by an abandoned sawmill at Coyote Spring. The vigilantes opened fire on the spot and Billy and his pals leaped for their horses. O'Folliard, Pickett, and Rudabaugh went humping down the creek hell-bent for freedom, but the ponies under Billy and Wilson were cut to the ground.

The two hard-pressed youths snatched out their rifles and dodged into the old sawmill. They paused for a moment to scatter the vigilantes with rapid fire, and then ducked out the back and took to the hills on foot, sticking to some old lava beds to cover their tracks.

Billy was sick over the death of his pony. It is said the horse he lost that day was the one John Tunstall had given him, Old Grey. The brave grey horse had seen a lot of action-packed mileage in its three years under Billy.

Tom and Pickett had made a clean getaway, but Rudabaugh had picked up a spare horse from a nearby farm and doubled back to find Billy and Wilson. Riding single and tandem the three men covered the thirty-five miles to a friend's ranch.

The rancher's name was Jim Greathouse and he had a great deal of admiration for Billy. He didn't understand why the law was so down on the Kid. Nearly every active participant in the Lincoln County War who still resided in the Territory had received a full pardon. But not William Bonney. It didn't make sense.

The following dawn ushered in December and the thermometer took another plunge. Flaky snow filled the pulseless air and spread itself thinly over the chilled ground. The vigilantes, now fifteen strong, circled Greathouse's ranch and stationed themselves behind convenient trees and outbuildings. They called upon the men inside the house to come out and surrender to the "law."

Billy asked "What law?" Were they a legally deputized posse? Were they carrying warrants for his arrest? The vigilantes had to admit no to both questions, which to Billy's mind made them nothing more than an armed mob out to pick up a little easy reward money. Billy and his two pals decided to show them it wouldn't be as easy as they had hoped. They refused to surrender.

The vigilantes didn't know what to do about that. They fired a few shots at the house but that didn't get them anywhere. Finally the ringleader, James Carlyle, said he would make a truce and go in and talk to the Kid. Billy was willing to listen to reason, so Carlyle went into the house. At the same time Jim Greathouse came outside to act as hostage until Carlyle returned.

The vigilante and the three outlaws sat down with a bottle of whisky to hold a pow-wow. According to Joe Steck (Greathouse's cook) Carlyle proceeded to get rather potted and surly, insisting upon immediate surrender. But Billy refused to turn himself over to a mob, knowing that lynch law was a popular practise in the West.

"You'll have to stay in here with us till it gets dark," he told the drunken man. "You'll be our hostage and lead our way out. We'll turn you loose once we're in the clear."

Carlyle had no choice but to remain where he was. Twilight came rapidly over the winter land, then darkness. The snow was still flutter-falling and the shivering vigilantes were growing apprehensive. What was keeping Carlyle? Finally they decided not to wait any longer. They would move in on the house under cover of night. At that moment one of them foolishly fired a shot.

"Good Lord," Carlyle gasped, "the idiots have shot Greathouse!"

It was a fatal mistake. Thinking that his men had killed Greathouse, thereby abolishing the truce and making *his* life a forfeit, Carlyle sprang to his feet and took a running dive at a window.

There was a great shattering of glass and wood and for one static moment Carlyle's hurtling body was pictured in the window frame. Instantly a discharge of shots roared in the night and James Carlyle flopped dead in the snow with three bullets in him.

That was enough for the White Oaks crowd. Licking their wounds, they rode off for home. That same night Billy, Wilson, and Rudabaugh set out to find the other two members of their band.

Who killed Carlyle? No one will ever know. Naturally the vigilantes said that Billy and his pals had shot Carlyle in the back; but Jim Greathouse said that the shots came from *outside the house*, and Joe Steck claimed the vigilantes had admitted to him that "it was all a mistake." Billy himself later stated that the White Oaks posse had mistakenly fired on their own men.

Needless to say the legend creators have never been able to settle for this. They prefer to have it believed that Billy alone fired the three fatal shots. How else can they add up the mythical tally of the twenty-one men he was supposed to have killed during his twenty-one years on earth? For some obscure reason it has always been of vital importance to American folklore that Billy the Kid should be accredited with the death of one man for each year of his short life. No one knows why.

It was because Billy the Kid was becoming a legend in his own time that Pat Garrett was so determined to capture him.

Why?

Perhaps it was a secret jealousy, or maybe it seemed to be a shortcut to fame. Certainly there were far more brutal and dangerous men running loose in the Territory at that time—although none were surrounded with that romantic and dramatic aura which Billy unconsciously wore like a stage cloak. In the three years since he had first entered the violent New Mexico scene he had managed to capture the avid imagination of the entire nation. He had become a symbolic figure.

Yes—it would be a grand feather in the cap of the man who finally brought down the notorious Billy the Kid. And Pat Garrett greatly coveted that elusive feather.

Doggedly he and his posse stuck to the cold gusty trails, casting right and left in ever expanding ring hunts; north to Las Vegas, west to Santa Fe, east to Anton Chico, south to Puerto de Luna (Gateway of the Moon) and Fort Sumner, and east again to Billy's famous cave hideout at Los Portales. To track down the Kid had become an obsession with Garrett. He was going to make this the most relentless manhunt in the history of the Southwest.

Billy and his band continued to move on ahead of the posse, shifting to the sides, doubling back, crossing their own trail, making a dry camp in the moaning hills one night, holing up in a friendly Mexican's adobe hut the following night.

A warrant was still in force against Charlie Bowdre for the killing of Buckshot Roberts, and out of a need for protection, he now rode with Billy again. He told his old sidekick that as far as the newspapers and law were concerned Billy was supposedly the leader of a large gang of notorious bandits who had murdered Carlyle in cold blood and who were perpetrating outrageous crimes from border to border.

What crimes? He had rustled some of Chisum's steers, which he figured he had coming, and the only shots he had fired since the night of July 19, 1878, had been in self-defense—the first at Joe Grant, the second at the White Oaks posse at Coyote Spring.

Incensed by Charlie's news Billy paused in his game of hare and hounds to write a letter to the governor, carefully explaining that he and his friends had been attacked by an armed mob and that Carlyle had been accidentally shot by his own men.

But it was too late; Wallace had already drawn his own conclusion about the Carlyle shooting. He posted a $500 reward for the apprehension and arrest of William H. Bonney, alias "the Kid."

That was that. Billy was now fairly certain that Wallace had no intention of keeping his end of the bargain to secure a full pardon for him. There is a tiresome legend that because of this he made the following vindictive vow:

"I mean to ride into the plaza at Santa Fe, hitch my horse in front of the Old Palace, and put a bullet through Lew Wallace."

And furthermore, that Wallace defiantly insisted upon making himself a target by sitting before an open window with a blazing lamp at his side while he wrote his immortal *Ben Hur*! Whoever dreamed

123

up this one overlooked the timing. *Ben Hur* had already been published by the winter of 1880. Anyhow, Billy was far too busy trying to dodge Garrett's posse to worry about a showdown with the governor.

The manhunt continued for two restless weeks, and then Garrett decided to try his hand at a little strategy.

A dance had been scheduled to take place at Fort Sumner in mid-December, and it was just possible that if Billy and his fun-loving riders thought the coast was clear they would try to attend it. So Garrett spread the false rumor that he and his men were pulling out for Roswell and, to give credence to the ruse, they set off for the south. But on the night of December 19 they quietly slipped into Sumner and stationed themselves around the old Indian hospital.

The trap was ready. Would the hare walk into it?

Sure enough, long about nine p.m. Billy led his little cavalcade down the snow-drifted Los Portales road. As they approached the old hospital Tom O'Folliard eagerly spurred on ahead of the others. Garrett and his thirteen hidden men leveled their rifles.

"Halt!" Garrett yelled, and at the same time he and Deputy Chambers blasted at Tom.

The lanky young Texan swung around in his saddle and slumped over his horse's neck. Billy booted his pony off the road and into the black shelter of a peach orchard. Dave Rudabaugh's horse went down in a blaze of guns—but Billie Wilson wheeled about, gave Dave a hand up, and they went pounding down the road riding tandem. Pickett and Bowdre were already long gone in the gusty night.

Tom O'Folliard's horse stepped toward the front porch of the hospital, bearing its sagging rider toward the possemen.

"Throw up your hands!" Garrett called.

Tom couldn't. A rifle bullet was lodged two inches

124

under his heart. "Don't shoot," he said. "I'm through."

Garrett's men helped the wounded boy from his saddle and carried him into the building. One of them brought him some water. Suddenly Tom gasped, "Oh my God, is it possible I'm gonna die?"

"Your time's short, Tom," Garrett said.

"The sooner the better then," Tom spoke his last words.

Outside Billy nudged his pony down the tree-shadowed aisle. He knew it was over. He had heard Tom say "I'm through." Suddenly his eyes pricked and filled with moisture. He had not been conscious of a similar weakness since the day his mother died. He had admired John Tunstall more than any other man—but laughing rollicking Tom O'Folliard had been his best friend. Nothing would ever seem the same again now. The wild, bold days of the Regulators were gone forever.

Billy joined the rest of his *compadres* at the Wilcox ranch some miles east of the fort. Neither the posse nor the outlaws could make a move the next day due to a heavy snowstorm; but on December 21 Billy's band pulled out of the ranch and headed toward Stinking Springs, and the posse left Fort Sumner to trail them.

There was not much to recommend Stinking Springs as a hideout. It was a barren, rock-ribbed, isolated place with a thread of creek gurgling through a shallow gulch. A doorless, one-room stone-built hut crouched on a bench above the ditchlike arroyo. The five dispirited outlaws crammed themselves into the icebox hut with two of their horses and spent a melancholy day and night huddling in their blankets for warmth.

Three hours before dawn Garrett's posse slipped along the arroyo on foot and strung themselves out in a prone line facing the front of the hut. Shivering and cursing the cold under their frosty breath, they waited for the tardy sunrise.

A pallid sun mounted wearily over the snow-white hills, and Charlie Bowdre came through the doorway with a feedbag for the three sorry horses hitched in front of the hut. Garrett gave him the same chance he had given Tom O'Folliard.

"Hands up!" he yelled, and two sudden rifle shots shattered the white silence.

Charlie dropped the bag, clutched his chest, and reeled back through the doorway. Billy caught his friend and held him up. He needed only one look at Charlie's torn chest to know that his old *compadre* was through.

"Don't put me down, Billy," Bowdre gasped. "Keep me on my feet."

Billy drew Charlie's Colt and put it in the dying man's hand.

"You're done for, Charlie," he said tensely. "Go out fighting. Go take one of 'em with you, *amigo*!"

Charlie staggered through the doorway and started to lurch across the open ground toward the staring men in the gulch. The pistol hung in his limp hand, blood dribbled from his mouth. No one spoke, no shot was fired. Garrett's spellbound men watched him stumble slowly toward them. He reached the edge of the ditch and paused. His mouth worked to form words.

"I wish— I wish—"

He toppled forward into the ditch and into one of the deputy's arms. No one ever knew what it was Charlie Bowdre wished.

Billy closed his eyes and leaned against the stone cold wall for a moment. Now they were all gone and he was the last of the Regulators. How had it happened? What had gone wrong? Why had everything worked against them from the very beginning? Then an exhilaration of fury swept over him. At least he would go out fighting. He reached through the doorway to get a grab on one of the halter ropes of the three horses outside the hut.

Garrett anticipated the move. Billy wanted to get two more horses inside the hut; then they could make a mounted dash for it in the dark. Garrett drew a bead, and just as the first horse stepped toward the door he fired a slug through the poor beast's heart. The horse collapsed in front of the hut, blocking the doorway. They couldn't possibly get their ponies over that obstacle.

"Hey, Billy!" Pat called. "How are you boys fixed in there?"

"Pretty well," Billy replied. "But we haven't any wood to make breakfast with."

"Plenty of it out here," Garrett said. "Come get some. Be a little sociable."

Billy laughed. "Can't do it, Pat. Business is too confining. No time to run around."

The mention of breakfast gave Garrett an idea, and he had some of his men build a cookfire to fry up a feed. He figured the heady scent of hot coffee and sizzling bacon would be a grand inducement for the four cold hungry men to surrender.

It was, but Billy didn't want to give in to it. He set to work to tunnel an escape hole through the stone wall in the rear of the hut. Garrett had anticipated that too, and a couple of deputies opened fire on the back wall. So that scheme was nipped in the bud.

Late in the afternoon Garrett started another parley.

"Better give up, Billy. You can't escape and you can only hold out in there so long. We'll get you sooner or later."

"If it sounds so easy to you, Pat—come on in and get me now!"

127

But he was alone in his resolve to fight his way out. The strain was too much for that tough *hombre* Dave Rudabaugh. He said he was cashing in and Pickett agreed with him. Billie Wilson wanted to quit but he waited to see what their leader would do. To his mind Billy the Kid was the greatest man who ever came down the pike.

Dave used his bandana for a flag of truce and he and Pickett came out of the hut unarmed. Billy looked at young Wilson who was watching him with an expectant expression. Perhaps he thought of all the eager young men who had once rallied around him . . .all gone now. He shrugged and dropped his rifle and walked out the door.

The following day Charlie Bowdre was buried beside his friend Tom O'Folliard at Fort Sumner. And Billy the Kid, the last of the Regulators, was placed in a wagon—manacled hand and foot—and was started on his way toward the Territorial jail in Santa Fe.

Chapter 12

On the afternoon of Christmas Day Garrett and a couple of his deputies brought their four prisoners into Las Vegas. Word had spread that the famous Billy the Kid was coming and a great unruly crowd had lined the street to greet him. Many of them cheered loudly when they saw the young outlaw in the wagon, but there were quite a few who called out veiled threats.

The prisoners were taken to the local calaboose for the night. Pickett, who was wanted for some minor charge, would remain in Las Vegas. The others, facing federal indictments, would proceed to Santa Fe. A reporter from the Las Vegas *Gazette* appeared at the jail to interview Billy. Rudabaugh was sullen and noncommunicative, and Billie Wilson was suffering from a sense of shame and would hardly lift his head. Billy the Kid, however, was in high spirits.

"You appear to take it easy," the reporter said to him.

"Sure," Billy replied. "What's the use of looking on the gloomy side of everything? The laugh's on me this time."

He glanced around at the dismal lockup and asked, "Is the jail at Santa Fe any better than this? This is a terrible place to put a fella in."

He kicked the toes of his boots on the stone floor to warm up his feet, and said, "There was a big crowd gazing at me today, wasn't there? Well, perhaps some of them will think me half a man now. Everyone seems to think I was some kind of animal."

When the reporter asked how he had become so notorious in such a relatively short time a shadow came over Billy's face.

"After the Lincoln County War I found there were certain men who wouldn't let me live in peace in this country. They say I'm a rustler, but I haven't stolen any stock. I made my living by gambling because that was the only way I *could* live. They wouldn't let me settle down. If they had, I wouldn't be here today."

He rattled the chains on his wrists, staring at them.

"Chisum got me into all this trouble and then wouldn't help me out. I went to Lincoln to stand my trial on the warrant that was out for me, but the Territory took a change of venue to Mesilla, and I knew that I had no show, and so I skinned out. Since then everybody's been after me, and there's no place I can stay."

The next day Garrett put Billy, Rudabaugh, and Wilson on the train to Santa Fe. An ugly mob had gathered at the depot to demand that the hated Rudabaugh, who seemed to have even more enemies than Billy, be turned over to them. Garrett and his deputies stepped out on the rear platform of the coach with their rifles.

"If you want him," Garrett said to the mob, "you'll have to take him from us."

The would-be lynch mob lacked a leader. They

were indecisive. Garrett went inside the coach to speak to his prisoners.

"Don't worry. If they try to mob us, I'll turn you loose with arms."

Both Rudabaugh and Wilson were in a nervous sweat, but Billy was grinning with excitement. "All right, Pat," he said. "Just hand me a six-shooter when it happens." Then he stuck his head out the window and looked at the milling mob.

"There ain't any danger," he said. "Those *hombres* won't fight."

He had judged them correctly. They were mostly noise. In a little while the engine hissed steam, gave a lurch and the wheels started to roll. Spotting his friend the reporter on the depot platform, Billy raised his manacled hands and lifted his hat.

"*Adios!*" he called gaily.

Billy was delivered to the Santa Fe jail on or about New Year's Eve. He had not been in this town since the time when his mother married William H. Antrim—eight years earlier, when he was young Henry McCarty. Unfed, he was chained to the bare floor of a stone cell, while Pat Garrett strode off triumphantly to file a claim for his reward.

Billy rotted in the drab Santa Fe cell for three long months before he was sent to Mesilla to face trial for the murder of Sheriff Brady. In that time he wrote four notes to Lew Wallace in the desperate hope that the governor would finally agree to live up to his promise. The first was dated January 1, 1881:

I would like to See You for a few moments if You can Spare time.

There was no answer. Billy sweated out two restless months and wrote the second note on March 2:

I wish You would come down to the jail and see me. It will be much to your interest to come (as) I have some letters which date back two years and there are Parties who are very anxious to get them but I will not dispose of them until I see you.

The letters he referred to were a part of the plan and agreement he and Wallace had made in 1879. Still the governor made no reply. Angrily, Billy wrote his third note on March 4:

I expect you have forgotten what you promised me two Years ago, but I have not, and I think You had ought to have come and seen me as I requested you to. I have done everything that I promised you I would, and You have done nothing that You promised me . . .it looks to me like I am getting left in the Cold. I am not treated right by (the jailer). he lets Every Stranger that comes to See me through Curiosity in to See me, but will not let a Single one of my friends in, not Even an Attorney. I guess they mean to Send me up without giving me any Show, but they will have a nice time doing it. I am not intirely without friends. I shall Expect to See you Sometime today.

Patiently Waiting

Three anxious weeks went by but there was not one word from the mute governor. Billy was running out of time. The coming Monday would see him heading for Mesilla, the trial, and the gallows. He wrote his final demand on March 27:

Dear Sir

For the *last time* I ask. Will you keep Your promise. I start below (Mesilla) tomorrow   Send Answer by bearer.

No bearer arrived at the jail because no answer was sent. Like Pontius Pilate, Governor Wallace had washed his hands of the entire affair.

On Monday Billy and Wilson were shackled together and given only a moment to say goodby to their sidekick Dave Rudabaugh.

"*La via esta duro, amigo.*" The road is hard, friend, Billy said.

They never saw him again. Eight months later Rudabaugh broke out of jail and fled to Mexico where, according to a widespread report, he was killed by a lynch mob in Sonora. Dave never was very popular.

U.S. Marshal Neis was in charge of the escort, and Billy's hated enemy Bob Olinger was his deputy. The little group proceeded to Las Cruces by way of rail. Dr. Hoyt, a one-time friend of Billy's recorded that he boarded Billy's coach for a minute when the train made a stop at Bernalillo.

"Is there anything I can do for you, Billy?" he asked.

The boy was wearing handcuffs and leg irons and Olinger was sitting across from him holding a double-barreled shotgun. Billy laughed.

"Sure, Doc. Just grab Bob's gun and hand it to me for a moment."

Olinger grinned crookedly. "Boy, you'd better tell your friend goodby. Your days are short."

"I don't know," Billy said, smiling. "There's many a slip 'twixt the cup and the lip."

How right he was.

From Las Cruces the two prisoners were carried by stagecoach to Mesilla and placed in a vermin-haunted jail. William Wilson's case was called first, on or about April 2, 1881. Wilson pleaded not guilty to the charge of passing counterfeit currency and his trial was scheduled for the next session of court. Everyone was eager to get to the main event: the trial of Billy the Kid.

Judge Bristol presided at this trial and his one aim was to see Billy the Kid at the end of a rope. He called the first case on April 5. This was the *United States of America vs. Charles Bowdre, Doc Scurlock, Hendry Brown, Henry Antrim, alias Kid, John*

Middleton, Stephen Stevens, John Scoggins, George Coe, and Frederick Waite in the shooting of A.L. "Buckshot" Roberts. Henry "Kid" Antrim was of course the sole remaining defendant.

Billy's court-appointed, and unpaid, attorney entered a plea of not guilty and asked that the indictment be dropped, arguing that the killing had not taken place on a federal Indian reservation as alleged, but at Blazer's Mill which was private property.

Judge Bristol possibly did not feel he was on sure ground with the Roberts killing. On the following day he dismissed the federal case, dropping all charges, in preference for the Territorial case which was obviously the real issue here.

On April 8 he called the case of the *Territory of New Mexico vs. John Middleton, Hendry Brown, William Bonney, alias Kid, alias William Antrim* in the shooting of Sheriff William Brady. Once again Billy was the only available defendant.

The prosecution produced three witnesses: Jacob "Billy" Mathews and George "Dad" Peppin, who had been involved in the shooting, and Bonnie Baca, who claimed to have seen the shooting from a distance. Billy's two old enemies, Peppin and Mathews, testified that the only man they had seen at the scene of the killing was William Bonney. No, they couldn't remember seeing Fred Waite in the street (even though one of them had shot Waite in the thigh); only Billy.

The defense could not produce a single witness except for Billy himself. He readily admitted he had taken part in the shooting, motivated by the information that Brady and his deputies had intended to ambush McSween, that he had been acting as a deputy under Special Constable Brewer, with a warrant for J.B. Mathews' arrest, and that he had fired only at Mathews and had missed him.

It was argued that at the time of the shooting a state of war had existed in Lincoln County, and that in a war the combatants were not supposed to be prosecuted for their participation. It was probably on this moot point that all of the indicted Murphy-Dolan men had received the governor's pardon.

But this bore no weight with Judge Bristol when it came to Billy's case. He refused to let the defense give to the carefully selected jury its final instructions which in effect said that Billy could only be found guilty of 1st degree murder if the evidence they had heard proved beyond a reasonable doubt that he had fired the fatal shot or shots, or had actually assisted in firing them with a premeditated design to kill Brady. In giving his own instructions to the jury, however, Bristol practically ordered them to bring in a verdict of guilty. His words, in part, were:

"If the defendant was present, encouraging, inciting, aiding in, abetting, advising or commanding this killing of Brady, he was as much guilty as though he fired the fatal shot. I have charged you that to justify you in finding the defendant guilty of murder in the first degree, you should be satisfied from this evidence to the exclusion of every reasonable doubt that the defendant is actually guilty . . . To justify a verdict of guilty it is not necessary for you to be certain that the defendant is guilty . . . Merely a vague conjecture or bare probability that (he) may be innocent is not sufficient to raise a reasonable doubt of his guilt."

With the judge's prejudiced admonition ringing in their ears the jury retired for a short while, then brought in the predetermined verdict: "Guilty of murder in the first degree."

Billy was not in the least surprised. For three years he had known that the Santa Fe Ring would go to any extreme to have him railroaded to the gallows. Quite stoically he listened to Judge Bristol read his death sentence on April 13.

William H. Bonney would be delivered to the sheriff of Lincoln County, and on May 13, 1881, he would be hanged.

A diehard legend persists in turning this somber scene into a wisecracking farce. According to the Upson-type mythologists Judge Bristol concluded his sentence with these words: "—where you will be hanged by the neck until you are dead, dead, dead." To which Billy promptly and cockily replied, "And you can go to hell, hell, hell." There is not a shred of evidence to substantiate this and the court records do not verify it.

Though not cocky, Billy was far from disheartened. He knew how to bide his time, wait for his chance and, when it presented itself, to act with swift daring. Meanwhile he cheerfully .put up with Bob Olinger's vindictive sneers and side-splitting jokes about "toedancing in the air at the Noose Fandango."

There was a good possibility that Billy would not reach Lincoln alive. *Newman's Semi-Weekly* newspaper was doing its best to prejudice its readers against the Kid, even trying to incite a mob to lynch him. A reporter from the Mesilla *News* interviewed him in jail on April 15, asking him what he thought about his chances.

"If mob law is going to rule," Billy said, "then we better dismiss judge, jury and sheriff, and let all take chances alike. I expect to be lynched in going to Lincoln." Then he grinned at the reporter. "Advise your readers never to engage in killing."

"Do you still expect a pardon from the governor?"

"Considering the active part Wallace took on our side and the friendly relations that existed between him and me, I think he ought to pardon me. Don't know that he will do it though." Billy shook his head. "I think it hard that I should be the only one to suffer the extreme penalties of the law."

On April 18 Billy was led from his cell by the three deputies who were to escort him to Lincoln. Considering the selection it is a wonder he made it alive. They were Bob Olinger, J.B. Mathews, and Kinney. Just one big happy family! He said goodby to his last friend, Billie Wilson, and hobbled out to the waiting wagon.

Within a few weeks Wilson tunneled his way out of jail and disappeared into Mexico. He was not heard from again for over ten years.

A large crowd gathered to see Billy shackled to the deputies' wagon. Someone asked him if he thought he could trust his guards.

"Oh sure," Billy laughed. "They won't hurt me unless somebody gives them a good excuse." He thought it was a standoff whether a vigilante gang lynched him or Olinger, Mathews, and Kinney shot him in the wagon. He didn't seem much concerned about it.

Actually Mathews and Kinney had relaxed their old animosity toward Billy now that he was definitely on his way to the gallows. Not so with Olinger; he was a vituperative as ever, doing his ornery best to break Billy's indomitable spirit. The four day trip gave him a fine opportunity to taunt the helpless prisoner.

When they stopped to eat, Olinger would suggest, "Better enjoy the meal, Kid. You don't have many more coming." And at night when they pulled into a stage station, he would say, "Why bother to sleep now? You'll be getting lots of it next month."

But he was wasting his breath. Try as he might he could not get a rise out of the condemned youth.

The little party arrived in Lincoln on April 21, and Billy was turned over to his erstwhile friend Pat Garrett. He had exactly three weeks to wait. Then he was scheduled to step into eternity on the end of a rope. Unless . . .

Chapter 13

The House of Murphy & Co. had collapsed as suddenly and quietly as a house of cards. Murphy was dead and Jimmy Dolan and John Riley had packed up and moved away. Their Pyrrhic victory in the Lincoln County War had utterly ruined them. The old Murphy store was now the new Lincoln courthouse and jail.

Billy was confined in the upstairs corner room where his friend Frank Coe had once been held. Garrett appointed Bob Olinger and a thirty-year-old Marylander named James Bell as Billy's round-the-clock guardians. Pat was taking no chances with foxy Billy; his guards were to remain in the same room with him twenty-four hours a day, only leaving him one at a time to get their meals at Wortley's Hotel across the street.

An old belief is still held that Deputy Bell was very charitable in his attitude toward the young prisoner, going out of his way to do him kindly little services, including admonishing Olinger for taunting the Kid about his approaching appointment with the gallows. This is rather doubtful when one considers the fact that James Carlyle—supposedly shot in the back by Billy—had been Bell's best friend. Bell had also been a member of the vigilante gang that had attacked Billy's little band at Coyote Springs. Just how "charitable" all this made him toward his prisoner must remain a matter of conjecture.

Billy's room was a large square chamber with a cot, three chairs, and a table against the east wall. A chalk "deadline" had been drawn down the center of the room and the two guards had been instructed to shoot the prisoner on the spot if he stepped over it. The adjoining room was Garrett's office, which opened into the hallway leading to the stairs.

Billy wore cuffs on his wrists (too tight this time to slip over his slender hands) and linked leg-irons on his ankles. There wasn't much for him to do during the warm dull spring days but to lounge around on his cot, roll cigarettes, and deal himself poker hands. The only exercise he got was when one of his guards would conduct him downstairs to the outhouse in the backyard.

He had no way of knowing that this outhouse was to play a very vital part in his predicament within one week.

Olinger continued to make his blowhard allusions about Billy's "necktie party," and thought it was a great joke when he tacked up a calendar in order to cross out the passing days. Each X on the calendar brought Billy that much closer to his rendezvous with Judge Hemp.

Many Mexicans desired to visit Billy in jail but Olinger would not allow it. The only visitor the prisoner could have was Godfrey Gauss, who had once been the caretaker of Tunstall's ranch; now he was the courthouse janitor. He and Billy discussed the good old days and current events like a couple of happy old gossips.

John Middleton, Gauss said, had supposedly died in Texas from the old chest wound he had received at Blazer's Mill. It was rumored that Hendry Brown had robbed a bank in Kansas and was apprehended and hanged. And Frank and George Coe had finally received the governor's pardon and were back at their Ruidoso ranches. He didn't know what had become of Doc Scurlock, Fred Waite, and Jim French.

That pretty well took care of the old Regulator bunch. Seven of them were now dead, five of them had disappeared, two had been pardoned, and one was sitting in the shadow of the Hanging Tree.

Olinger gleefully continued to cross off the days on the calendar: April 22, 23, 24, 25 . . .

About April 26 Sam Corbett, who had been the clerk in Tunstall's store, dropped in to see Billy. Olinger was over at the hotel at the time and Bell had no objection to the visit as long as Corbett was unarmed. Corbett had carefully stayed out of the bloody feud of 1878, and perhaps he was now motivated by a sense of guilt for not having taken an active side with the McSween-Tunstall faction.

There is no proof of this, but it is the general belief of most Lincoln County War scholars and historians that Corbett had written a note to Billy which was folded in a small square and concealed in the palm of his hand when he stepped up to the deadline to shake hands with the prisoner.

Billy said nothing except goodby to Sam, and returned to his cot to roll a cigarette. Bell was reading a newspaper and Billy covertly unfolded the note and glanced at its contents. Corbett had hidden a Colt in the crossbeams of the outhouse roof.

Billy raised his manacled hands to take a drag on his cigarette, and popped the note into his mouth and swallowed it.

The opportunity had now presented itself but the

time for swift action must wait. A man got only one chance like this in a lifetime. No sense in muffing it by rushing. Billy casually smoked his cigarette and contemplated the fat lazy flies on the ceiling.

Thursday, April 28, arrived and Billy glanced at the calendar on the opposite wall. He had been in this room exactly one week. In fifteen days he was due to take that short but very final walk to the scaffold.

Garrett came into the room and announced that he was off to White Oaks to see about collecting the county taxes, telling his two deputies that he would be back on Saturday. Billy sat on his cot with a pokerface. He had been counting on just this.

It is said the following conversation took place:

"Don't ever let the Kid see the back of your shirts," Garrett warned the two guards. "Keep your eyes on him every minute."

Olinger patted his double-barreled shotgun.

"I got a total of eighteen buckshot in here," he said, "and if the Kid stops either one of them loads he'll feel it plenty."

Billy grinned. "Better take care you don't catch a load of buckshot yourself, Bob."

This sounds almost too prophetic to be true; but in any event Garrett took off for the north and Billy settled down to give him a good head start. He had already laid his plans—now it was just a matter of timing.

Noon rolled around and Olinger stood up, stretched, and announced he was going over to the hotel to get his lunch. Supposedly he halted by the calendar and grinned back at Billy.

"Ain't I the careless one? I forgot to mark off the day for you, Kid. Why didn't you remind me?"

"I mean to remind you, Bob," Billy said with a cryptic smile.

141

Olinger gave a gruff laugh and penciled an X over the figure 28.

"Fifteen days to go, Kid, till the thirteenth. Say—thirteen's an unlucky number, win't it?"

"That's what I've always heard, Bob," Billy replied.

There were three other prisoners confined in the building for petty offenses and it was Olinger's duty to conduct them to the hotel for their chow. But he didn't need his shotgun for that. He leaned the gun against the wall by Bell, telling his partner to keep an eye on it.

Billy pretended not to be aware of the shotgun across the room. He swung his chained legs up on his cot, placed his handcuffed arms on the windowsill and stared down at the somnolent sun-bright street. He watched Olinger and the prisoners cross the dusty road and enter the hotel. Then he put his feet down and stood up, and asked Bell to take him downstairs to the outdoor privy. It was everyday routine and Bell thought nothing of it.

Billy hobbled across the room, crossed Garrett's office, shuffled along the hall and went clinkity-clank down the stairs with Bell right at his back. The time for a tigerlike move was now.

He hopped into the warm adobe outhouse and closed the door, leaving Bell waiting outside in the glaring sun. Urgently his manacled hands fumbled along the tops of the timber beams. Suddenly his groping fingers felt a small bundle wrapped in newspaper. He snatched it down and drew out a loaded Colt. Good old Sam!

Billy pushed open the door, stepped outside and poked the gun in Bell's back. It was siesta time in the lazy little town. Not a soul was in sight. He told Bell that he didn't want to hurt him; all he had to do was lead the way upstairs and behave himself while they waited for Olinger to return. He probably intended to lock Bell in an upper room and then get the drop on Bob when he came up the stairs.

The two men—Bell leading, Billy close behind with the cocked Colt—reentered the building and went slowly up the stairs. It was when they reached the upper landing that Bell made his fatal mistake. He suddenly whipped around took a wild swing at Bill's head—missed—and went leaping down the stairs. Billy swung his manacled hands and jerked off a snap shot when Bell was halfway down.

The bullet socked the adobe stair wall at an angle and ricocheted into Bell's chest. Dead on his feet and not knowing it, Bell stumbled out the side door and toppled into the arms of the startled janitor, Old Man Gauss.

Billy hadn't meant to kill the fool Bell but he was far too keyed up at that moment to worry about it. Anyone might have heard the shot. Jamming the Colt in his belt he went hop-hop down the hall, through the outer office, and into his cell and snatched up Olinger's shotgun. Then he leapfrogged over to the side window and looked down at the sunny road.

Olinger, in the hotel, had heard the shot and dropped his fork in shocked surprise.

"Good Lord, Bell's shot the Kid!"

He rushed outside with his pistol in his hand and trotted across the road toward the old Murphy store. Billy, standing just behind the upper window, watched him come. Olinger started to approach the front of the building, calling, "Bell? Bell?"

He must have sensed that something was wrong because he abruptly changed his mind and turned toward the east corner to take the pathway to the side door. Obviously Billy would have no chance now to get the drop on Bob and disarm him. Olinger was set to blast first and ask later. Awkwardly Billy took a sight with the shotgun.

"Hello, Bob," he said in a quiet voice.

Olinger slammed to a halt and snapped up his head. He saw the twin barrels of his own shotgun staring down at him like glaring black eyes. One of the barrels went *CA-BALOWM* and Bob Olinger was thrown flat on his back and straight into eternity. In an overwhelming passion of hatred Billy fired the other barrel, and then pitched the empty gun out the window.

"Take that with you where you're going, Bob!" he yelled.

He heard someone running and he quickly fumbled the Colt out of his belt. Old Man Gauss was trotting along the east side of the building. He stopped short when he spotted Olinger's crumpled body.

"Don't run," Billy called down. "I won't hurt you. Find me a file—and hurry!"

Gauss nodded distractedly and ran. Billy wasn't out of the woods yet; there was still a lot to be done. He hopped through Garrett's office and out onto the front balcony. So far only a few men had gathered in the street. They were standing in a huddle before the hotel, gawking at the courthouse and at the youth up on the balcony with the six-shooter in his shackled hands.

"All you *hombres* stay where you are!" he shouted at them. "I'll shoot anybody who tries to get out of town."

None of them seemed inclined to make a move. Jumping like a kangaroo Billy went down the hall to the arms closet by the head of the stairs. It was locked but he burst the door by throwing his full weight against it.

There was quite an array of weapons and he made his selection with some deliberation, just as if he were shopping in a gun store. He chose a new Colt, holster and gunbelt, and a Winchester rifle, and

144

took the time to fill two spare cartridge belts with shells; not an easy job while wearing handcuffs.

Hopping over to the nearest window he saw Gauss down in the backyard. The old man was so rattled he was nearly running in circles. He called to Billy that he couldn't find a file anywhere. The best he could do was a small pickaxe.

"Toss it up," Billy ordered. "Then go through Bell's and Bob's duds and find the keys to these blasted bracelets."

Hop-hop-hop along the corridor again and back out on the balcony. One of the idlers across the street who had more curiosity than sense had just started to walk toward the courthouse. Billy yelled at him to get back if he knew what was good for him. He did.

Billy was actually sitting fairly pretty. There was only the one road going through town; from the west end was the only way to reach Fort Stanton—and he commanded this exit from his lofty perch on the balcony.

Old Man Gauss, shaking as if he had palsy, fetched up the key and Billy finally rid himself of the detestable handcuffs.

"You go and saddle me a mount," he told the old man, "and I'll clear out as soon as I can loosen the shackles from my legs."

It took him nearly an hour of sweating and straining to snap the rivet on the left leg shackle. That was more like it. At least he had one leg free and could walk and ride like a man again. No time to waste on the other leg. He cinched up the long chain and lashed it to his belt to keep it out of his way.

More and more spectators were gathering across the road now, all watching Billy's exertions in spellbound silence. It is said that after he snapped his shackles he did a short triumphant dance-step for them on the balcony. No one in the crowd offered the slightest resistance, even though anyone could have easily picked him off with a pistol. Most of them were on his side and wanted to see him make a clean getaway.

Armed like a pirate, Billy jingle-janked downstairs and went out the side door. Sam Wortley had ventured across the street to offer some help because old Gauss seemed to be having an awful time trying to catch and saddle a skittish pony in the old Murphy corral. Billy looked at Bell's body laying just outside the door.

"I'm sorry I had to kill him," he told Sam, "but couldn't help it." Then he walked over to the sprawled Olinger and gave him a nudge with the tip of his boot.

"Bob's not going to round me up again," he said quietly.

Poor old Gauss was near to having heart failure with the unruly pony who would bolt first one way, then the other. Gasping and steaming and windmilling his skinny arms, the doddering old fellow worriedly called to Billy that he would get the brute in a minute.

"That's all right," Billy said. "Take your time."

They say he leaned against the wall and calmly rolled a cigarette as he watched old Gauss with some amusement.

Finally the pony was caught, saddled, and a pair of blankets were tied behind the cantle. Gauss led the horse into the street and Billy walked out and swung into the saddle. His clattering chains spooked the pony and it promptly bucked him off.

Billy picked himself out of the dust with a grin and handed Gauss his Winchester. He swung aboard again and this time the pony stood still. Billy reached for his rifle.

"Whose pony is this?" he asked. "I'll send it back to him tomorrow."

"Belongs to Billy Burt, the county clerk," Gauss told him.

Billy nodded and raised his rifle, waved at the smiling spectators. One of them wished him good luck.

"*Gracias, amigo*," Billy replied.

He started out of town at an easy canter. A little Mexican boy was the last to see him go. He said Billy the Kid was whistling happily as he joggled into the west.

Chapter 14

Billy rode through purple sage and stands of pinon trees and across grassy meadows, staying clear of the Bonito river road. Fort Stanton was only nine miles away, and once they got the word some troopers would probably ride out to trail him. But he seldom worried about the pony soldiers; they were lousy trackers.

His biggest concern was the leg-irons—that and Pat Garrett. When Pat learned of his escape he would come highballing down from White Oaks like a tornado. He swung off to the right and splashed across the sun-golden stream at Baca's ford and selected a canyon trail among a crazy crosscut of huge stone gullies.

He was at home in this wild land, following an off-trail path that was a continuation of the Capitan Gap. The pony picked its way nimbly up the rising trail, mounting to the top of a gradually swelling slope that was capped by leaning, ruined crags, some wind-rounded, others rain-wrinkled.

Billy pulled up and turned in the saddle to look back at the distant little town which in a sense he had made nationally famous. It was his last view of Lincoln.

Twilight was coming to meet him as he urged the pony down into a walled amphitheater. He had Mexican friends living in these isolated hills and he rode to the little adobe home of Jose Cordova. The surprised Cordova sent his son to fetch Billy's old *compadre* Hijinio Salazar, the boy who had played dead on the night of July 19, 1878.

The two Mexicans went to work on Billy's leg-irons, knocking them off in short order with a hammer and chisel. True to his word Billy wrote a note to the county clerk and tied it to the pommel of the pony's saddle. Reputedly the note read:

Billy Burt—You would cry if you lost your horse. I won't need him any more. I am sending him back to you. Much obliged. Give Pat Garrett my regards.

Turning the pony's head toward Lincoln he slapped the horse on the thigh and watched it gallop riderless on down the draw. Old Man Gauss was stunned when the pony trotted into town early the next morning and came to a halt at the courthouse corral. He hadn't believed that Billy meant to keep his promise.

That same night the loyal Salazar paid a moonlight visit to a nearby rancher's corral and relieved one Andy Richardson of a powerfully built mustang named Don. Billy didn't have a cent to his name to make this right but it has been authenticated that he later asked his friend Pete Maxwell to pay Richardson for Don, and Billy would settle with Pete when he could scare up the cash.

Ironically on that same April date Governor Wallace gave an interview to a reporter from the Las Vegas *Gazette*. It was in regard to Billy the Kid's death sentence.

"It looks as though Bonney will hang," the reporter said.

"Yes," Wallace replied, "the chances seem good that the thirteenth of May will finish him."

"He appears to look to you to save his neck."

"Yes," Wallace said with a smile, "but I can't see how a fellow like him should expect any clemency from me."

Billy wasn't expecting any. He had taken care of the matter himself, and now he was rambling north for Fort Sumner. Wallace didn't learn of this startling development until the following day, and he immediately posted a reward bulletin:

BILLY THE KID
$500 Reward

I will pay $500 to any person or persons who will capture William Bonney, alias the Kid, and deliver him to any sheriff of New Mexico. Satisfactory proofs of identity will be required.

Lew Wallace
Governor of New Mexico

This should have been a grand incentive to get Sheriff Garrett hot on the scent of the famous fugitive. Not so. For some reason he appeared to have lost his spunk. He hung fire in Lincoln for a number of days, apparently in a deep mood of irresolution. He had ordered the lumber for Billy's scaffold, and now that it was on hand there was no Billy to hang. Instead he had to use the lumber to make coffins for his two dead deputies! It galled Pat that everyone thought this was a dandy joke on him.

U.S. Attorney Tom Catron had taken over Dolan's cattle on the Pecos and now he and his erstwhile enemy John Chisum had a common bond of fear. They wondered if Billy would try to gun them down or simply satisfy himself with raiding their cow camps. They fervently urged Garrett to get the lead out of his breeches and go find the outlaw. But Pat still couldn't seem to shake himself from his lethargy, and many people began to murmur that he was afraid to face the Kid in a showdown . . .

Instead of heading north where he would become the number one living target for any lawman or bounty hunter, Billy should have turned south for Old Mexico and safety. Certainly he was aware of this as he cantered into the sandhill approach to Fort Sumner, but he had already decided against it.

For one thing he was flat broke and he couldn't live in Mexico on jawbone; he believed in paying his own way. For another—and a far more vital reason —he was beginning to be haunted by his own legend. If he quit now they would call him a coward, and he couldn't live with that. And why *should* he quit? What right did they have to force him out of the Territory when he had fought long and hard for his right to stay there?

No, he wouldn't run out. And if they refused to let him live in peace, then they would have to come for in arms. He would never again submit to shackles and jail and the shadow of a noose. No surrender. They would have to shoot him down as they had Tom and Charlie.

The thirty-one static days of May passed away and June came in blistering hot. The lonely young outlaw and his big bay mustang lived in the solitary hills like a mute pair of doomed souls. They rambled somberly under towering overhanging walls, in and out of light and shadow, along the bright piñon-splattered slopes, and followed chuckling little streams that seemed to meander aimlessly toward some enigmatical destiny.

They drifted, alone and without a purpose, the horse seemingly content to plod forever into nowhere, the rider wistfully dreaming of the bold young days when he and all his *compadres* had fought for a cause that had gone down the drain.

On cold nights Billy would hole up with a Mexican friend. The *pobres* he could always trust, but he could never be sure of any *gringo*. One night way down on the Rio Peñasco two young line riders were eating their spartan meal in an isolated little cabin. When they suddenly looked up Billy the Kid was standing in the doorway with his rifle in his hands.

"Well," he said, "I got you, haven't I?"

John Meadows and Tom Norris were common cowboys, not gunhands, and they were frankly scared out of their wits as they gawked at the most notorious badman in the Southwest.

"Well," young Meadows managed to say, "so you have. So what are you going to do with us?"

Billy smiled and lowered his rifle. "I'm going to eat supper with you." And he sat down and helped them with their beans.

They talked about the Lincoln County War, and finally Meadows asked Billy what he thought of Pat Garrett.

"If I was hiding in an arroyo with a gun," Billy said, "and Pat rode by and didn't see me, I wouldn't hurt a hair on his head. He worked pretty rough to capture me, but he treated me good after he got me. I don't hold any grudge against him."

Meadows, who developed a profound and lasting liking for the friendless twenty-one-year-old outlaw, warned him he had better stay clear of Fort Sumner or Garrett would get him sure as shooting.

Billy shrugged. Where else could he go? Fort Sumner was like home base to him. He was irresistibly and inevitably drawn toward the place. It was his Trail's End.

One of the more prevailing legends that surrounds Billy the Kid concerns a rather vague Fort Sumner señora who through the passing decades has been identified as Celsa Gutierrez.

152

Legend has it that she was the young wife of an elderly Mexican, from whom she was separated at the time and she was deeply in love with the picturesque young outlaw who was desperately fighting his hopeless battle against insurmountable odds. Accordingly it is said that it was because of this girl that Billy was finally drawn back to the old army post. Whatever the actual reason might have been, it is known that Billy was on intimate terms with Señora Gutierrez, and he did return to Fort Sumner early in July.

One of the first things he did was talk to Pete Maxwell about Richardson's horse. Aside from asking Pete to settle with Richardson, he also made a request which strongly indicates that he realized his time was nearly up . . .

If something should happen to him—if he were killed—would Pete promise to take good care of Don for as long as he lived? The horse had been his only friend for two months and was like a brother to him.

Pete Maxwell solemnly promised to do as Billy asked. He never went back on his word. Hardy old Don lived a life of exalted ease for many years at Fort Sumner.

Ten weeks had now passed since Billy had blasted his way out of the Lincoln jail, and still Garrett made no move to start the manhunt. To his thinking Billy had surely lit out for Mexico, and with such a lengthy head start what hope did a posse have of tracking him down? None. So why waste the energy?

Uncle John and others, fearing for their very lives, did not agree with this apathetic thinking. As far as they were concerned Billy was waiting behind every tree, rock, and corner with a rifle in his capable hands. They were quite vehement in their demands that the sheriff *do something*—at least make an attempt to catch the Kid.

But Garrett could not be budged. Perhaps he *was* afraid; perhaps not. Possibly he simply did not know where to start looking. Then he found out late in the second week of July . . .

Deputy Sheriff John Poe, stationed at White Oaks, received a visitor one night in his hotel room. The caller was a man with information regarding the whereabouts of Billy the Kid (some would have it believed that this nocturnal informer was none other than Celsa's jealous husband Señor Gutierrez).

The informer's story was short and sweet. Through a thin partition in a livery stable he had heard two cattlemen (supposedly the brothers Sam and Dan Dedrick, friends of Billy's) say that the Kid was in Fort Sumner and had been for some days.

Deputy Poe immediately rode posthaste to Lincoln and told Pat Garrett the news. Pat shook his head, saying, "I don't believe it. Billy has more sense than to hang around there!"

Poe agreed with him but suggested they ride up there just to be sure. What could they lose by it? Garrett said all right, but to his mind it was just a wild-goose chase.

The two lawmen went by way of the Hondo to Roswell, where they picked up another deputy, one Tip McKinney. In McKinney's opinion there was as much chance of Billy the Kid being in Fort Sumner as there was of him being in the moon. Still and all Garrett had to make some show of activity, if only to satisfy the influential cattlemen who had helped him become county sheriff.

The highly skeptical three-man posse headed north on July 10. There was no great rush and they arrived in the sandhills below Fort Sumner on July 13, just as dusk was stealing across the Pecos. They holed up in a dry gulch for the night.

Come morning they discussed their plans over iron rations. One of them should meander into the fort and see what news he could pick up. Garrett was too well known at the old army post, and McKinney said so was he. That left it up to John Poe.

Poe hitched his pony outside Beaver Smith's saloon around noon and slouched into the bar pretending to be a down-at-the-heels prospector from the Capitans. A gang of idle wranglers asked him how were pickings, and he told them pretty punk. Then he casually brought up the ever-popular subject of Billy the Kid.

Instant silence fell over the room and the wranglers stared at him with glowering suspicion. Obviously Poe wasn't going to learn anything from this bunch. He made a diplomatic retreat and rode north to Milnor Rudolph's ranch. This Rudolph had once been a member of Garrett's posse, but now he was suddenly playing dumb. No, he hadn't seen or heard about the Kid; he believed that Billy had pulled out for Mexico. It wasn't any of his business anyhow.

Rudolph's evasiveness aroused Poe's suspicions. The man was afraid of something. He rode over to La Punta de la Glorietta, four miles north of Sumner, and found Garrett and McKinney waiting for him in a stand of cottonwoods.

"From the way Rudolph and those other *hombres* acted," Poe said, "I'm sure they know the Kid's somewhere around here."

Garrett was still dubious. Billy wasn't the sort to skulk in the sagebrush when he could be gambling in a saloon. But as long as they had come this far they might as well play out the hand.

"We'll slip into town tonight and have a talk with Pete Maxwell," Pat said. "He's a friend of mine and maybe he'll tell me the truth. Maybe."

Now it was the night of July 14, 1881, and the three lawmen quietly approached Sumner from the north. They pulled up at the woodslike peach orchard, dismounted and ground-hitched their ponies, and then slipped through the dark orchard until they reached a point where they could observe the empty parade ground and the row of old adobe barracks. They hunkered down among the little fruit trees to look, listen and wait.

Two hours dragged by. It was nearly midnight. A small group of Mexicans were lounging on a porch across the road, conversing softly. One man stood up and said *Adios* and walked down the row of adobe buildings, past Pete Maxwell's house, and disappeared. He was too far away for the three hidden men to make him out.

The two deputies were tired and wanted to call it quits for the night. The Kid wasn't going to show up. Garrett felt the same way, but said he would just have a word with Maxwell first. They cut through the orchard and went down the Lincoln road to the back of Pete's house, and then across the side yard. Pete's bedroom was the corner room facing a roofed porch.

"Wait here," Garrett murmured.

He stepped onto the porch, opened Pete's door, and entered.

Poe and McKinney drifted over to the fence that fronted the old parade ground and leaned against the gate posts. Even Poe was ready to admit that the whole affair looked like a washout. Billy was probably long gone to Mexico just as they had originally figured.

Neither of them realized that they had actually seen Billy the Kid only ten minutes before.

Chapter 15

A sultry summer moon was on the rise when Billy jogged out of the east on Don. The arid mesa lay silvery and forlorn in the moonlight, the rims flattened and in places became hardly more than rolling ridges. He approached Sumner at an easy lope and pulled up, scanning the darkened village between dust-caked lids.

Everything looked all right—sleeping peacefully.

He moseyed past the little adobe-walled cemetery where his two pals were at rest, and he felt a heavy dullness of despair. He was beginning to dread the empty loneliness of his hunted existence. He could take it all right if someone like Tom were still with him, but going it on his own hook this way was wearing his spirit thin.

Seventy-eight days he'd had of it now . . .

He trotted by the abandoned hospital and halted just beyond the old Indian corral to hitch Don to a crumbling shack. Then he walked across the parade ground and joined a few Mexican friends having a quiet chat on a darkened porch. He didn't stay long. It was getting on to midnight and he was trail weary.

He stood up and one of the Mexicans said *buenas noches* to him.

"*Adios*," Billy said. He walked along the picket fence, past Pete's house, and crossed the open ground to Celsa's home.

She must have known that he would come to Fort Sumner that night because she was waiting up for him. Billy went inside and tossed his hat on the table, hung his gunbelt and holster on the back of a chair and sat down and pulled off his boots. He was bone tired. It was mighty fine to stretch his toes and sit in a chair in a cozy room like a human being for a change.

"Beelie," Celsa said worriedly, "you must not stay here. It is not safe for you. You must go to Mexico."

Billy shrugged. He no longer seemed to care. Maybe he would go. *Quién sabe?* Right now he was too bushed to worry about it. He just wanted to rest awhile. How about Celsa frying him a steak?

Celsa said she had no meat in the house, but there was a freshly killed heifer hanging in Pete's meat house. She would start the fire if Billy would go slice off a steak for himself.

Billy yawned and stood up, drew his double action .41 Colt and tucked it in the front of his pants. Then he picked up a butcher knife and stepped outside.

Walking noiselessly in his stocking feet he went along the inside of the picket fence toward Pete's house. He crossed the yard and stepped onto the porch—and heard something scuff in the dirt by the fence.

His left hand snatched at the Colt as he swung to the right. The black figures of two men were standing in the gateway. They seemed as surprised to see him as he was to see them. But the shadow-ribbed moonlight was tricky and they couldn't make him out.

"*Quién es?*" Billy hissed. Who is it?

Poe and McKinney were leaning negligently on the gate posts like a pair of drowsy horses. They mistook Billy for a Mexican sheepherder; plenty of them lived in the old fort.

"Take it easy," Poe said in a reassuring voice. "We're not going to hurt you."

Billy didn't like the setup one bit. Who were those two strange *gringos*? What were they doing in the fort at that time of night? He backed away slowly, still covering the two mildly bewildered men with his Colt. Then he stepped through the doorway into Pete's bedroom—into the trap that had been set by pure chance.

Pat Garrett was sitting on Pete's bed on the other side of the room in the pitch dark. Pete was in the bed and Garrett had been questioning him when he suddenly heard Billy's voice outside on the porch. At least he had *thought* it was Billy's voice. He pulled his pistol, placing his left hand on Pete's chest to keep him still.

Not daring to breathe, his ears straining for the slightest sound, he heard Poe's voice—"We're not going to hurt you." And a moment later he saw the silhouette of a bootless man slip into the room.

Billy still had the moonlight in his eyes as he entered the black room and he was as blind as a bat. But he was well acquainted with the arrangement of the furniture in Pete's room and tiptoed toward the bed, lowering the Colt to his side.

"*Quiénes son estos hombres afuera*, Pete?" he whispered. Who are those men outside?

This time Garrett was positive it was Billy's voice. But he seemed to be caught in a daze of suspended animation. It had all happened too quickly, too unexpectedly; it had thrown his libido out of gear. Trancelike he watched the barely discernible figure of the man in stocking feet come closer to him.

"*Quiénes son?*" Billy repeated. Who are they?

159

What on earth was wrong with Pete? Why didn't he answer? Suddenly Billy froze. Someone was sitting on Pete's bed only three feet away! He was certain of it.

"*Quién es?*" he hissed at the mute figure.

He didn't know what to think. Why didn't the fool answer? He started to back off. He could have blasted the man where he sat, but he didn't because for all he knew it might actually be Pete. It was his fatal mistake. He played fair to the end, giving the mystery man a chance to speak up.

Garrett never spoke a word. He whipped up his pistol and pulled the trigger and threw himself to the left, to roll clear of the bed.

Billy saw a brilliant flash and the blackness exploded with a stunning roar as some powerful unseen force propelled him backwards—back, back into a shimmering glassy abyss. He never saw the second shot Garrett fired from the floor.

Pete Maxwell left the bed in one jump and raced for the door with Garrett right after him. The two startled deputies were coming rapidly along the porch and they nearly shot Pete in their bewildered excitement. Garrett apparently was even more unstrung than his deputies.

"That was the Kid who came in there on me!" he yelled at them. "I think I got him! I've killed the Kid!"

Poe couldn't believe it. "You mean that sheepherder? Pat, I think you got the wrong man."

"No," Garrett insisted. "I know his voice. I'm certain it was Billy!"

A handful of sleepy-eyed Mexicans gathered in the dark yard. They, like Poe, couldn't believe that "Beelie" was really dead. No one wanted to go into the dark death room and find out for sure. The unnerved lawmen had a good reason for not volunteering. Suppose it actually was Billy the Kid in there, and suppose Garrett had missed him?

Finally old Deluvina Maxwell, a Navajo woman who had been adopted by Lucien Maxwell when she was a child, came along the porch with a lighted candle. She said nothing, giving Garrett a contemptuous look, and walked into Pete's room alone.

Billy the Kid was laying on the floor on his back, his open eyes staring up at the ceiling. Garrett's first bullet had hit the boy just under the heart, killing him before he had reached the floor. Pat's second wild shot had been at a washstand in another corner of the room.

Cautiously the three fearless lawmen came into the room with their pistols drawn and ready. Garrett claimed that Billy had fired at him in between his two shots, but the others doubted it because they had heard only two shots.

Poe picked up Billy's Colt and broke it open. There were five loaded chambers in the cylinder and one empty shell, but the empty was an old shell that had been fired days before.

Old Deluvina glowered at Garrett and cursed him in Spanish, calling him four kinds of coward. She had looked upon the gay young *caballero* as a wayward but fond son; and Garrett had shot him down like a dog—in the dark without a chance! Nor was it the first time, she spitefully reminded him. He had called to Tom O'Folliard to halt, and had promptly shot him dead. He had ordered Charlie Bowdre to put up his hands, and had instantly shot him. *Pobrecitos!* Poor little ones, she cried.

Pete Maxwell walked out of the room dejectedly. He was sick to the bottom of his soul. Billy was gone. Somehow he had never quite believed it would happen. Even with all the odds against him Billy had always appeared to be invincible.

He crossed the parade ground, looking for Don in

the dark. It was time to live up to his promise to Billy. He heard the scuff-scuff of a restless hoof pawing at the dirt and followed the sound around behind the old adobe barracks. The big mustang was standing impatiently in the shadow of an abandoned hut.

Pete stroked Don's muscular neck for a moment, then unhitched him and led him across the lot to the big Indian corral. He freed the saddle, slipped off the bridle and gave the horse a slap on the rump. The big bay mustang took off around the corral in a spirited free-running lope, as frisky as a colt.

Pete watched him go off into the moonlight, listening to the thuppity-thup of his throwing hoofs. Then he leaned against the top rail and lowered his head. Now the last one of all those wild young *hombres* who had jauntily rode forth three and a half years before to avenge Tunstall's death was gone. Tomorrow Pete and his friends would have to bury Billy beside his two *compadres*, Tom and Charlie.

And that would be the end of it.

Don trotted back across the corral toward the saddened man, and came to a halt in the bright moonlight. He lowered his Roman nose and went pawpaw at the silvery dust. Then he began to swing his head from side to side as if disagreeing with the man.

The last of the Regulators would ride on forever.

Postscript

A perusal of the actual facts makes it relatively easy to explode the myth of the "twenty-one men, not counting Mexicans and Indians," Billy the Kid supposedly killed. Of the famous "twenty-one" sixteen have been identified as Windy Cahill, the Negro trooper at Fort Union, Bill Morton, Frank Baker, William Brady, George Hindman, Buckshot Roberts, Bob Beckwith, Morris Bernstein, the three Chisum riders, Joe Grant, James Carlyle, James Bell, and Bob Olinger. Let us take them one at a time and see how many were positively killed by Billy.

There is no doubt that he killed Cahill.

There is no evidence that a Negro soldier was killed in Fort Union, or that Billy was ever near the place. In any event Fort Union is in northeast New Mexico, and he would have been four or five hundred miles away (either in Arizona or Old Mexico) at the time of the alleged shooting.

He was present at the Morton and Baker shooting and probably fired at them, but how can he be given the sole credit for their deaths when they were struck by *eleven* bullets?

Certainly he was involved in the Brady and Hindman shooting, but those two men were hit *twelve* times, and even Pat Garrett later said that he doubted if Billy had fired at either of them, knowing that Billy really only wanted to get Mathews.

All the eyewitnesses affirmed that Charlie Bowdre shot and killed Buckshot Roberts.

It is generally accepted that Billy killed Bob Beckwith when he made his dash from McSween's house, but it has never been proved. At the time of the shooting some twenty men were firing as rapidly as possible in the flame- and smoke-filled night, and Beckwith was standing in the middle. Anyone's bullet might have hit him.

All the eyewitnesses declared that Antonio (Atanacio) Martinez killed Bernstein. Martinez himself not only admitted it, but offered to stand trial for the shooting.

The shooting of the three Chisum riders is pure hogwash. It took place only in the mind of a myth spinner.

Billy definitely killed Joe Grant.

Here is a statement made by one Buck Saunders a few weeks after the Carlyle shooting: "Me and two other fellows were ordered to go out (to Greathouse's ranch) and plant Jimmy. We found him frozen plumb stiff. When we turned him over, we saw he had been hit in the chest by several bullets. If Billy had killed him, the wounds would have been in the back because he was running like hell to get away from the place. When we came back, we told (Deputy Sheriff) Hudson what we seen, and he got hostile. He said to forget it, for we didn't see nothing like that, and we must have been feeding on loco weed or been plumb snowblind . . . Now that I'm stampeding out of this here Territory for Texas, I'm telling you for certain, the Kid didn't kill Jimmy Carlyle."

There has never been any doubt that Billy killed

Bell and Olinger.

Thus out of the sixteen identified men from the mythical "Twenty-one" we come down to a positive four who were actually killed by Billy's hand: Cahill, Grant, Bell, and Olinger—the first two in self-defense, the second two while breaking out of jail in order to avoid being hanged for a crime which he probably had not committed. This hardly sounds like the bloody record of a "smiling, psychopathic killer."

But the legend workers have never concerned themselves with the bare bones of the facts, and I rather imagine they will continue to propound the Legend of Billy the Kid for a long time to come. As Walter Noble Burns, the greatest myth weaver of them all, once said: "As each narrative adds a bit of drama here and a picturesque detail there, one wonders what form these legends will assume as time goes by, and in what heroic proportions Billy the Kid will appear in fireside fairy tales a hundred years or so from now."

One indeed wonders.

Robert Edmond Alter

News Items Relating to
Billy the Kid's
Early Life

Much of the mystery surrounding Billy's early life stems from his having had too many names. For years historians tried to uncover information on William H. Bonney, a purely fictitious name, and their lack of success was what prompted many writers to fill the gap with their own so-called facts. Had they known that Billy was actually Henry McCarty (later Henry Antrim) much of the ensuing confusion could have been avoided. A knowledge of the following news items certainly would have helped to establish his early whereabouts and activities . . .

The Grant County *Herald*, October 1875:
Henry McCarty, who was arrested on Thursday and committed to the jail to await the action of the Grand Jury upon the charge of stealing clothes from Charley Sun and Sam Chung, celestials, sans cues, sans Joss sticks, escaped from prison yesterday through the chimney. It's believed that Henry was simply the tool of "Sombrero Jack," who done the stealing whilst Henry done the hiding. Jack has skinned out.

The Arizona *Citizen*, August 22, 1877:
Austin (sic!) Antrim shot E. P. Cahill near Fort
Grant on the 17th inst. and the latter died on the
18th. Cahill made a statement before death to the
effect that he had some trouble with Antrim during
which the shooting was done. Deceased . . . was born
in Galway, Ireland, and was aged 32. The coroner's
jury found that the shooting "was criminal and unjustifiable, and that Henry Antrim, alias Kid, is
guilty thereof."

The Mesilla Valley *Independent*, September 1877:
On Monday last, three horses belonging respectively
to Col. Ledbetter, John Swishelm and Mendoza,
were stolen from Pass coal camp in the Burro Mountains. On learning the fact Col. Ledbetter and Swishelm went out to the camp and trailed them in on the
road at Apache Tahoe. Sometime on Tuesday the
party of thieves, among whom were Henry Antrim,
were met at Cooks Canyon by Mr. Carpenter. Telegrams have been sent to Sheriff Barela at Messila,
and we hope to hear of the arrest of the thieves and
the recovery of the horses.